CHRISTMAS PERIL

HAZARDOUS HOLIDAY

LYNN SHANNON

CHRISTMAS PERIL

Copyright © 2022 by Lynn Balabanos

Published by Creative Thoughts, LLC

All rights reserved.

No part of this book may be reproduced in any form or by any electronic or mechanical means, including information storage and retrieval systems, without written permission from the author, except for the use of brief quotations in a book review.

This book is a work of fiction. Names, characters, businesses, organizations, places, events and incidents either are the product of the author's imagination or are used factitiously. Any resemblance to actual persons, living or dead, events, or locales is entirely coincidental.

Cover design by Maria Spada.

Scripture appearing in this novel in whole or in part from THE HOLY BIBLE, NEW INTERNATIONAL VERSION®, NIV® Copyright © 1973, 1978, 1984, 2011 by Biblica, Inc.™ Used by permission. All rights reserved worldwide.

Glory to God in the highest heaven, and on earth peace to those on whom his favor rests.

Luke 2:14

ONE

An icy wind ruffled Noelle Logan's hair as goose bumps rose on the nape of her neck.

Something about this place didn't feel right.

It was too quiet. Like a ghost town.

Her boots crunched over gravel in the parking lot. Samson's Nursery was a plant store located on the outskirts of town on an old country lane that dead-ended into the place. The air was scented with a mix of flowers and mulch. Pretty strands of white lights dangled from post to post, chasing away the deeper shadows created by the encroaching nightfall. No one was at the front counter.

Noelle fought against the desire to hop back into her SUV and leave. She'd been driving for the last ten hours from Memphis to spend the holiday with her grandmother. Exhaustion seeped into her muscles. She wanted a hot meal, a shower, and a warm bed. In that order. But she'd promised to stop and pick up a Christmas tree for her grandmother. Sheila Logan was pushing eighty-five, and while the older woman was spry and active, she couldn't manage hauling an evergreen into the house alone. She had a neighbor to help unload the tree, provided Noelle could pick it up on the way. The flower shop/Christmas tree farm was a simple twenty-minute detour.

It was a small favor. One Noelle was happy to do.

Except... except this place was sending off all kinds of strange vibes. Noelle couldn't quite pinpoint what was wrong, but something just felt off.

"Hello?" Noelle called out. A small building enclosed on only three sides served as a checkout station. It was decorated with a garland wreath and bright red bows. She rang the bell sitting on the front counter several times, the noise ringing out across the nursery.

No one appeared.

The sense of unease buried low in the pit of her stomach grew. Another frigid wind whipped across the open space, sending leaves and pine needles scattering across the gravel. The cold bit into Noelle and her shoulders rose up instinctively. This wasn't how she wanted to start her first vacation in years. The rapid pace of her career with the FBI had eaten away at every aspect of her life. She didn't have any friends outside of the agency, and dating was a distant memory. She was lonely and questioning her life choices. Some rest, hot chocolate, and stress-free holiday fun with her grandmother were exactly what she needed to reset.

This didn't feel very stress-free though. Noelle was exhausted and getting hungrier by the minute.

"Hello? Anyone back there?" She checked her watch and then the posted times on the counter. The place should be open. The register was sitting on the counter, change still in the tip jar.

There were more Christmas trees farther into the store. Maybe the owner was helping another customer back there. Her SUV was the only vehicle in the lot, besides a beat-up truck with the letters Samson's Nursery etched across it. But what other explanation could there be? Whoever was in charge hadn't been abducted by aliens.

Her cell phone rang. Noelle fished the device out of the pocket of her wool overcoat, glanced at the caller ID, and answered. "Hello, Granny."

"Hi, dear." Sheila's voice was cheerful. "I called to see how Operation Christmas Tree was going. Make sure you pick one of the short, fluffy ones. The ceiling in my living room isn't very high."

"I remember." Noelle backed away from the front counter and headed down the main aisle, deeper into the nursery. The sound of a mixer whirling came over the line. "What are you making?"

"Mashed potatoes. I prepared your favorite for dinner."

Her mouth watered automatically. "Meatloaf."

"Yep, with green bean casserole, mashed potatoes, and my famous biscuits. We've also got chocolate pie for dessert." Happiness filled Sheila's voice. "It's not every day my only granddaughter comes to spend Christmas with me. I intended to spoil you rotten."

Noelle's heart lightened. No one made her feel more special than Granny. It had been a long time since she'd spent the holidays with her grandmother. Far too long since she'd even visited. Growing up, and well into her teens, she'd spent every summer in Cutler, Texas. Since graduating from college and joining the FBI, Noelle hadn't been back. Her job was grueling, and vacation days were reserved for brief visits to see her parents in Nashville.

Granny normally traveled to Nashville too, but this year, Noelle's parents were trekking around Europe for the holidays. Her brother was buried in snow and legal briefs in New York. That left Noelle and her grandmother to spend Christmas together. It would be a quiet but wonderful holiday. She was truly looking forward to it.

But first, a Christmas tree.

Noelle switched the cell phone to her other ear and paused in front of an aisle of evergreens. She fingered one of the branches. "I'll be there soon, Granny. You have a neighbor that will help us unload the tree, right?"

"Oh, yes, dear. I also invited him for dinner. David Carpenter. You remember him, don't you?"

Noelle smiled, thinking of her first love. "David? I haven't seen him in ages."

They'd become friends during Noelle's visits to town. The summer between their junior and senior year of high school had shifted that friendship into a sweet teenage crush. But life and opportunity had separated them. Different colleges. Divergent careers. They'd drifted apart as a result. Still, Noelle had nothing but fond memories of the teenage boy who she'd shared her first kiss with.

"He's a police officer now," Sheila continued. "When I told him you were coming for the holidays, he was excited about the prospect of reconnecting. I hope you don't mind. In my opinion, it's always good to have a connection with people who knew you when you were young."

"I don't mind. I'd love to see David again and catch up

on what he's been doing." Thunder rumbled in the distance. Noelle glanced up at the sky. Clouds blocked the stars and moon. "I'd better let you go, Granny. I'll be there soon. Can't wait to see you."

"Okay, dear. Drive safe."

Noelle promised she would and hung up, craning her neck to see if the store clerk was tucked away in the Christmas trees with another customer. No one was visible, but the faint murmur of voices carried.

Finally. People.

Noelle adjusted the scarf around her neck to ward off the chill as a drop of rain peppered her head. Thunder rumbled in the distance. She'd better select a tree quickly before the storm unleashed.

A crack of lightning blazed across the sky. She picked up her pace, going deeper into the aisle lined with Christmas trees. "Hello? Anyone back here? I could use some help—"

Something whispered behind her. Noelle whirled just as a man-sized shadow burst from the collection of trees on her right. The attacker tackled her, sending Noelle careening into the opposite aisle of fragrant firs. The branches and needles jabbed her skin. She struggled to free herself. Adrenaline shot through her veins.

The attacker pounced, dragging her to the ground. Noelle punched out. He grunted as her fist made contact with his shoulder. She didn't stop. With a fury, she struck again. Her concealed handgun was holstered at the small of her back under her shirt and jacket. Utterly useless, since she couldn't reach it. Heart pounding, she relied on hand-to-hand combat training, but her position was weak. She was facedown on the ground. The attacker was on her back, squeezing the air from her body.

Stars danced across her vision. With increasing horror, Noelle realized she was about to pass out. Then he tangled his fingers in her hair. With a yank, he pulled her head back.

The cold metal of a knife touched her throat.

TWO

David Carpenter steered his police-issued SUV into the parking lot of Samson's Nursery. He radioed in his position to dispatch. This was the last stop of his shift. Margaret Samson, the owner, had called and requested he stop by at closing time. She needed to speak to him about an important matter, but insisted it happen in person.

The cryptic phone conversation had plagued him all afternoon. Margaret was down-to-earth and an introvert who preferred the company of plants to people. But her tone in the call had been stressed. David couldn't imagine what had upset the older woman, but he sent up a silent prayer that he'd be able to help.

Protecting the citizens of Cutler was an honor and a privilege. His hometown had faced new struggles in the last decade. Rapid growth coupled with a growing drug trade had changed the sleepy Texas haven to one in need of a strong police force. Chief Aiden James, David's boss and friend, had risen to the occasion. Cutler was still a safe place to raise a family, and the residents shared a strong sense of community. David wanted to keep it that way.

Wind scattered leaves across the gravel parking lot and brought with it the scent of pine. Christmas trees of every shape and variety stood at the entrance. More were in the rear. Samson's was the only place to buy a real tree for thirty miles. David noticed the unfamiliar SUV parked at the other end of the lot. His gaze snagged on the Tennessee plates.

Noelle? It was possible. She was driving in to spend the holiday with her grandmother. Sheila had requested his assistance in unloading the Christmas tree this evening and promised dinner in return. David had agreed.

It'd been almost ten years since he'd seen Noelle. He remembered her as a fun-loving and sweet teenager with a stubborn and independent streak. She was a piece of his childhood and his first love. Although time and distance had separated them, he'd followed her career with the FBI from the sidelines and was proud of all she'd accomplished. It was a bit nerve-racking to think of seeing her again though. She'd followed through on her dream of a high-octane law enforcement career. He'd taken another route. A more boring one.

Dependable David. That's what his last girlfriend had called him, the inflection in her tone suggesting that his dependability was a deficit. Maybe it was, but he didn't know any other way to be. Responsibility, integrity, and following through on commitments were unchangeable parts of his personality. Caroline had found him dull. She wasn't the first girlfriend who'd accused him of being a humdrum, but for some reason, her rejection had hurt the most. Maybe because he'd thought—with her—he'd found something special. A foolish notion.

Lightning flashed across the sky, followed by a low rumble of thunder. A pebble of rain dropped on David's bare head. He'd left his cowboy hat in the car. He adjusted the duty belt at his waist and picked up his pace. Margaret wasn't standing behind the front counter as usual. She must be helping the unknown customer with the Tennessee plates. Probably in the Christmas trees.

David strolled past lines of poinsettias. The sound of a scuffle reached his ears, followed by a woman shouting. "Stop or I'll shoot!"

Concern bolted through him. What on earth was going on? David unholstered his weapon but kept it pointed at the ground. He didn't want to harm someone who had a rightful reason to be on the property. Was it a robbery? Possible. Although the register at the front counter had been closed, the tip jar filled with change.

David quickened his steps. The only illumination in this area of the shop came from rows of tiny white lights above his head. Deep shadows heightened his tension. They were big enough for a person to hide in. A row of toppled trees caught his attention, and he moved closer.

Someone stood in the dark. Adrenaline shooting through him, David pivoted in the aisle with his weapon raised. "Police! Don't move!"

"David?"

His heart skittered at the familiar voice. He lowered his weapon as Noelle stepped into the light. Her curly hair was tousled, pine needles tangled in the strands. Dirt coated her jeans and coat. A scratch marred the delicate curve of her cheek. Blood dripped from a slice along her neck, half hidden under the multicolored scarf wrapped around her throat. She had a handgun in one hand.

Shock tightened the knot in his stomach. He closed the distance between them in three strides. "What happened?"

"I was attacked by an unknown male." Noelle's fingers drifted to the cut along her throat. "He threw me into the trees and tried to slice my throat, but my scarf prevented him from being able to gain access to my carotid."

Her tone was flat. Professional. As an FBI agent, Noelle had likely been in many life-and-death situations. Still, David noticed the way her hand trembled. A buried desire to comfort his childhood friend rose up, but he pushed it aside and focused on his job. A man willing to slice a woman's throat needed to be off the streets. "Where did he go?"

"I fought him off, and he must've heard you coming, because he bolted that way." Noelle pointed westward toward the woods lining the property. "I gave chase, but he had too much of a head start."

"There's a farm road on that side of the property. Probably parked his vehicle there. Did you get a look at your attacker?"

"No." Frustration bled into her voice. "It was dark and everything happened so fast. Male. Around 6'0 give or take. Fit. That's not much to go on."

No, it wasn't. David radioed in the information anyway and requested backup to the scene. Then he turned back to Noelle. "Where's Margaret?"

She frowned. "Who?"

"The owner. Margaret Samson."

She inhaled sharply. "I don't know. No one was at the front counter when I arrived. I heard voices back this way and thought she was helping a customer. Then I was attacked."

David's muscles tensed. His gaze swept the immediate area, taking in the fallen Christmas trees and the scuffs in the dirt. Fear for Margaret bounced through him. He removed a flashlight from his duty belt and flipped it on. "I need to find her."

"I'm coming with you." Noelle's tone brooked no argument. "I'm a trained law enforcement officer and you need backup. We have no way of knowing if my assailant is the only one on the property."

She had a point. Still, David hesitated. "You're hurt."

"My pride is injured more than my body. I can't believe he got the jump on me." Fury sparked in her expression. She dropped her hand from her neck. "I'm fine. Just scratches. Let's find Margaret."

David nodded his assent, then swung his light down the aisle. Leading with his weapon, he swept the next two sections, Noelle right behind, silently watching his back. They moved in tandem as if they'd always worked together. It was a strange feeling, one that would've unsettled him if his attention weren't locked on finding Margaret. The rain picked up speed, peppering them. An icy chill raced down his spine. He strained to hear any noise, but the nursery was as silent as a grave.

In the third aisle, the flashlight beam bounced off a flash of color.

David's gut clenched as he hurried forward. His cowboy boots crunched against the gravel as approaching sirens wailed in the distance. Margaret Samson lay on the ground. Blood coated her clothes from what appeared to be multiple stab wounds. Her eyes gaped open, unseeing. It was too late to save her, but David still checked for a pulse anyway.

None. Her skin was still warm to the touch.

Noelle stood near Margaret's feet, staring down at the woman. "My God."

David rose. "Now we know why you were attacked." Rage pooled in his belly, churning like a hornet's nest. "You witnessed a murder."

THREE

Morning sunshine streamed through the gauzy curtains in the guest bedroom. Noelle checked the alarm clock on the bedside table and groaned. After nine. She was normally an early riser, but the attack last night and the discovery of Margaret Samson's body had caused a restless night's sleep. Her mind wouldn't stop turning over the events, straining to remember any detail that might help bring the killer to justice. To no avail. She'd finally drifted off around daybreak.

Noelle tossed aside the covers. The scents of coffee and vanilla wafted under the crack of her closed door, lifting her spirits. Her grandmother was also an earlier riser. And a baker. Visions of cinnamon rolls, scones, and muffins danced through Noelle's head. She hurried through her morning routine and hustled into the kitchen. Then slid to a stop.

David sat at the kitchen table. He was dressed in a pressed Cutler Police Department uniform. The fabric followed his broad shoulders and contoured along the muscles. Clean-shaven, the sharp line of his jaw and cheekbones were on full display. A tan cowboy hat was hooked on the chair next to him. The faint indention from wearing it ran through his sable brown hair.

A shocking bolt of attraction burst through Noelle. The teenager she'd once dated had turned into a handsome man. A rush of memories flooded over her. Sharing ice-cream sundaes, running through fields at the Carpenter ranch, rocking on the porch swing under a thousand stars.

David offered her a charming half-smile, his gaze drifting over her sweatpants and T-shirt, before lifting to her face. "Morning."

Her cheeks heated. Noelle fought the urge to fix her hair. She'd tossed the mass of curls into a messy bun before coming downstairs. Her clothes were wrinkled, because she'd used them for pajamas. No makeup. Not exactly the way she'd envisioned running into her ex again.

Then again, last night hadn't been stellar either. At least now they weren't standing over a dead body together. Besides, who cared how Noelle looked? It wasn't like she and David were dating. They'd shared a dozen kisses and a childhood friendship. Nothing more. She was being silly.

Sheila, dressed in slacks and a reindeer sweater, pulled a sheet pan loaded with cinnamon rolls out of the oven. Her white hair was fluffed into a cloud that fluttered around her face, and she wore her signature pink lipstick. "Good morning, Noelle. There's fresh coffee, and if you give me five minutes to whip up the icing, these rolls will be ready to eat."

"They smell fantastic." Noelle kissed her grandmother on the cheek before pouring herself a cup of coffee. She carried the carafe to the table and topped off David's mug as well. "Is there any news about the investigation?"

"There is, although I'll give you a chance to drink some coffee before filling you in." His smile kicked up a notch, and Noelle's heart beat skittered. "Sheila says you think better after caffeine."

She laughed lightly. It was true. Noelle could function without her morning cup of coffee if necessary, but life was so much better with it. She took a sip of the dark brew. It was flavored with hints of caramel and chocolate. Noelle hummed her approval. "Granny, this coffee is amazing."

"David brought it." Sheila beamed in his direction before drizzling icing on the cinnamon rolls. "For you."

Noelle's gaze narrowed as her attention shifted from her grandmother to David. She sensed a plan was afoot and hoped Granny wasn't matchmaking. She'd spent some time last night chewing Noelle's ear off about David and made a point to say the handsome lawman was single.

The last thing Noelle needed at this moment was a romantic entanglement. Especially with a man who didn't live in the same state. "Hmmm. Seems the two of you have been talking about me."

Sheila's brow crinkled. "Only good things, dear. David came over early this morning to clear some branches that'd fallen in the yard during the thunderstorm, and I asked if he had any coffee. I completely forgot to pick some up at the store yesterday. He was kind enough to bring some over."

Oh. That made sense. David always had a special soft spot for Sheila. Removing the branches from her yard was just like him. Even at seventeen, he'd been thoughtful and kind. Her grandmother was also a tea drinker who didn't keep coffee in the house. Noelle took another long sip of the brew. "Thank you, David. This is perfect."

His smile widened. "You're welcome, although I got the better end of the bargain. Sheila's cinnamon rolls are the best in three counties."

"None of that malarky, young man. Your mother has won the annual pie baking competition four years in a row." Sheila plopped the cinnamon rolls in the center of the table and patted David's shoulder. "But I appreciate the sentiment."

David shook his head and chuckled. "I don't give false flattery. Mom's pies are the best, but you hold the trophy for cinnamon rolls."

Sheila laughed. "All right then." She handed out a plate to Noelle and David. "Dig in before they get cold."

The house phone rang. Sheila bustled from the room to answer the call. The low murmur of her voice filtered into the kitchen. Noelle chose a cinnamon roll closest to her. The freshly baked dough was soft, the warm scent of cinnamon and sugar enticing her senses. After discovering Margaret's body and giving her statement to David, Noelle hadn't been able to eat much dinner.

She quickly said a prayer of thanksgiving before breaking off a piece of the roll and popping it in her mouth. "Wow. Granny knocked it out of the park."

"I know. So good," David said, around his own mouthful. He took a sip of coffee, his hand giantlike compared to the mug, and eyed her speculatively. "How are you doing?"

She was tempted to shrug off his concern, but something about the genuineness in his question stopped her. Noelle sighed. "I don't know. I've been an agent with the

FBI for over seven years. You'd think, by now, I'd be used to murder, but something about last night..." She'd been haunted by the image of Margaret's body lying on the gravel. No one deserved to be killed and left like a pile of trash.

Noelle picked at her cinnamon roll. "I know it's an active investigation, but is there anything you can share?"

"There was almost no physical evidence recovered from the scene. Margaret was stabbed using some kind of sharp object—probably a knife—which the killer took with him." David frowned. "My boss, Police chief Aiden James, notified Margaret's sister last night. Kylie and Margaret worked together at the nursery, along with Kylie's husband, Brian. The family was devastated."

Noelle winced. Death notifications were never easy. "I wish I remembered more about what the attacker looked like. It's so frustrating to be on the sidelines."

"About that. I have a proposition to make. Our police department is short-staffed, and considering the lack of evidence we have on this case so far, I could use some assistance. You have extensive experience working these kinds of investigations. Any help you could provide would be appreciated."

Surprise rippled through her, followed by a rush of motivation. Noelle desperately wanted to bring the killer to justice. "I'd have to clear it with my boss, but I don't think it'll be a problem." Then she winced as guilt pinched her. "I'm supposed to spend the holidays with Granny."

"Don't worry about me, dear." Sheila came back into the kitchen, her soft-soled shoes silent against the tile floor. "We'll have plenty of time together. Catching Margaret's killer is important." She sat in a chair and patted Noelle's arm. "Besides, you have crime fighting in your blood. There's no use denying it. You'll just spend your time thinking about the case anyway."

Her grandmother was right. As usual. Noelle had already spent most of the night analyzing the case. She couldn't help it. Her father, Marcus, had retired last year from the FBI after serving for over four decades. He'd trained her early on to think like an investigator. Following in his footsteps, becoming a part of the FBI, had been Noelle's dream for as long as she could remember.

It was troubling to think about how unhappy she was in her job now. Noelle hoped and prayed it was momentary. Something in her life needed to change, that much was certain, but she wasn't sure what. Maybe working alongside David would help her figure things out.

David lifted his brows. "What do you say, Noelle? Want to help me catch a killer?"

"Absolutely." She straightened her shoulders. "Where do we start?"

"With Margaret's ex-husband."

FOUR

An hour later, David pulled into the parking lot of the Barzilla, a local honkey-tonk within spitting distance of Main Street. It was popular with townsfolk who overlooked the shoddy building in pursuit of a good time. At this hour of the morning, in the brilliant sunshine, the place was downright drab. Gray paint peeled from the exterior walls and wooden picnic tables were chained together on the front porch.

Noelle wrinkled her nose. She'd changed from sweats into a professional button-down shirt and dark slacks. Her curls were tied back into a neat ponytail. Just a hint of mascara and blush decorated her face. "It doesn't look open. How are we going to speak to Waylon Jennings?"

Waylon was Margaret's ex-husband. David killed the engine. "He lives above the bar. Margaret got the house in the divorce. Her sister said it's one reason Waylon was angry with her."

"How long were they married?"

"Three years. No kids. Waylon isn't from around here.

He moved to Cutler about five years ago and opened the bar. He's got a long rap sheet though. A couple of DUIs, arrests for assault and domestic abuse."

Margaret had been stabbed to death. The killer had taken the murder weapon—likely some kind of knife—with him. Had he found it at the nursery? Or did he bring it with him? David didn't know. But typically, stabbings were personal. An act of rage. Waylon's criminal record proved he had a problem with his temper.

David undid his seat belt. "On the day she was murdered, Margaret called me. She insisted I stop by the nursery and speak to her at closing time, that it was an urgent matter."

"And you have no idea what she wanted to discuss?"

"None. She wanted to talk in person." Regret swamped him. "Now I'm left wondering if that's the reason she was killed. I wish she'd told me what it was about." His gaze locked on the dingy bar. "Margaret and Waylon had a rough divorce. According to Kylie—that's Margaret's sister—Waylon held a grudge against his ex-wife. Maybe Margaret wanted to ask about a restraining order."

Noelle nodded. "It's a good thought. Let's see what Waylon has to say for himself."

They exited the SUV. Water from last night's thunderstorm stood stagnant in the potholes. The temperatures had warmed slightly, but the air was still frosty. David settled his cowboy hat on his head. Waylon's motorcycle was parked in the first spot. Sunlight glinted off the chrome.

Noelle jutted her chin toward it as they passed. "The killer escaped last night using the farm road along the edge of the property. Did the crime scene technicians recover any tire tracks?"

"Unfortunately not. The thunderstorm washed them away."

It was another frustrating fact about this case. There was almost no physical evidence. It was one of the reasons David had invited Noelle to work the case with him. She had extensive experience in difficult investigations and was an expert at interrogating witnesses. Her career with the FBI was stellar.

It took several knocks on the front door of the bar before Waylon answered. His thinning hair—more gray than brown—stood on end. He wore a T-shirt with the sleeves hacked off that displayed muscles earned through regular workouts. The scent of beer and cigarettes poured off him.

Waylon blinked at the bright sunshine like a mole coming out of his den. "Whaddaya want?"

David made the introductions and then said, "We need to speak to you about Margaret. May we come in?"

The other man scowled but backed away from the door, allowing them to enter. The smells of beer and cigarettes intensified, mingling with the faint odor of fried food. If Noelle recognized Waylon as her attacker, it didn't show in her expression.

The bar owner leaned against a stool and crossed his arms. "I figured you'd be coming by. Customers were talking about her murder with me all night."

David wasn't surprised that news about Margaret's death had spread so quickly through Cutler. Gossip was rampant and several members of the public, including the owner of the local newspaper, monitored police radio communications. Thankfully, the chief of police had notified Margaret's next of kin about the murder before anyone else did.

Noelle's gaze narrowed. "You don't seem upset about Margaret's death."

"We all grieve in our own way." Waylon removed a pack of cigarettes from the pocket of his shorts. "My process involved drinking a whole lot last night. I'm sorry she's dead, but our divorce was finalized last year and our marriage was over long before that. We were never a good match from the start."

"Why is that?"

He shrugged. "She was straight-laced. Her idea of a good time was grafting rose bushes together to make a new species. I don't know the first thing about plants. Booze, music, and people. That's what I like." Waylon fired up his cigarette and took a long drag. "Truth is, the ruin of the marriage was my fault. My dad was dying when I met Margaret. He was something of a plant guy too and had known her for years. We met and... I don't know. I was going through a hard time and Margaret supported me. We had something of a whirlwind relationship. Eloped. Things fell apart pretty quickly thereafter."

David rocked back on his heels. "Rumor has it, your divorce was nasty."

Waylon glowered. "Suppose Margaret's sister told you that. Kylie never liked me." He took another drag on his cigarette. "Listen, I had nothing to do with Margaret's death. I was here at the bar all night."

"Can anyone verify that?"

"Dozens of patrons and my staff. Ask around."

Noelle pointed to a camera hanging from the ceiling. "What about your surveillance footage?"

"It don't exist. Those cameras are just for show." Waylon yawned. "I gotta get back to bed. Y'all see yourselves out."

With that, he marched through a door on the left marked private, leaving a trail of smoke in his wake. The staircase creaked as he climbed to the upper floor. A door slammed above them. The interview was clearly over.

David and Noelle went back into the sunshine and climbed into his SUV.

"That was interesting." Noelle snapped on her seat belt. "I don't think Waylon is losing any sleep over his ex-wife's death."

"Me either. I'll follow up with his bartender and staff." David tapped on the steering wheel. "It's only a fifteen-minute drive to Samson's Nursery from here. Thirty minutes round trip. Even if Waylon was on site most of the night, that doesn't mean he couldn't have slipped out and murdered his wife. He's interacted with the police enough to know how to create an alibi."

"Good thinking." Noelle shot him an appreciative glance. Sunlight caressed the curve of her cheek. She was the type of woman who grew more beautiful with every passing year. "Sorry, but I don't think you need my help on this case at all."

Warmth flooded his chest at the compliment. "It never hurts to have another set of eyes and ears."

David drove through the center of Cutler. Main Street was decked out for the holidays. Red ribbons encircled the old-fashioned street lamps. A banner announcing the annual Christmas tree lighting in the main square was hung from the corner of the police station to the mayor's office on the other side of the road. Santa danced in the antique store on the corner, and a sign outside Gracie's Diner promoted their famous hot apple cider.

"I'd forgotten how pretty the town is." Noelle sighed and leaned back in the seat. "Especially during Christmas time. It looks like something out of a storybook."

"Yeah, it does. The spring is nice too. There's a flower fair on Main Street in May that draws people from nearby Austin. Good for the shops and business." David glanced at her. A faint bruise on her cheek reminded him of the grave circumstances that'd brought them together. Margaret's murder. His hands tightened on the steering wheel. "We've had an uptick in crime, but murders are still rare thankfully."

"Do you spend most of your time giving speeding tickets?" She tossed him a playful smile that reminded him of summer days and swimming in the river running through the state park. A time when they were both young and carefree. Noelle hadn't just been his first love, she'd been a part of his teen years.

He grinned back. "No, I don't just give speeding tickets. We have problems with drugs and the occasional theft. Tractors and cattle are big commodities in rural areas and there's a black market for them."

"Well, next time I work a stolen tractor case, I know who to call."

He rolled his eyes. "Yeah, yeah. Okay. It's a bit Mayberry, I grant you, but I can't imagine the kinds of cases you deal with regularly. Doesn't the stress ever get to you?"

"It does." The smile melted from her face, and Noelle sighed again. "Things have been rough for me these last few years. My job gives me purpose, but it also prevents me from having a life. I always thought I'd get married and have kids one day, but I don't even have time to date. Or have friends. Lately... I've been drained."

Suddenly, she looked exhausted. Her shoulders curled inward, her complexion pale. David stopped at a red light and turned to face her. "Hey, I'm sorry. You're on vacation. It never occurred to me that you'd need a break from work—"

"No." Noelle shook her head. "I want to help. Besides, Granny was right. If I'm not working the case with you, I'll just be fretting about it. It's better to be productive." She pointed to a coffee shop on his right. "I could use more caffeine though. Mind making a stop on our way to the police department?"

"Not at all." The light turned green, and he carefully maneuvered into a parking spot across the street from the Ground Bean since the ones in front of the store were already taken. David quickly circled the vehicle to open Noelle's door for her. "Word of warning, this place has the best desserts."

"Ugh, I'm going to gain twenty pounds during this trip." Noelle rubbed her flat stomach. "But there will be no regrets."

"None whatsoever." He grinned down at her. "Besides, you're stunning no matter what."

The words were out of his mouth before he recognized their implication. David's neck heated.

Noelle's eyes widened and her mouth gaped open

slightly, but she recovered quickly by lightly slapping his chest. "As Granny would say, stop that malarky. You were laughing at my pajamas and messy hair this morning."

Actually, he'd thought she'd been even more beautiful then. Fresh-faced and casual. But saying so would only dig him deeper into the hole he'd already created. David wiggled his eyebrows to tease her. "That's not true. I was simply impressed with your ability to wear a Tom and Jerry shirt at your age."

"Tom and Jerry are classics." She huffed, spinning around and marching toward the crosswalk before tossing a grin over her shoulder. "Come on. I need help to pick the best dessert."

David chuckled and shook his head. He hit the button on his fob to lock the vehicle as the crosswalk signal turned green. Noelle stepped off the curb into the street. Her gorgeous curls bounced with every step.

The rev of an engine caught David's attention. A large truck was barreling down Main Street, going far too fast, with no sign of slowing for the red light. David's heart skipped several beats as his gaze shot to Noelle centered in the crosswalk. His feet moved before his brain could fully form the next thought.

The truck was going to hit her.

FIVE

"Noelle!"

The panic in David's voice stopped her midstep. She turned to look in his direction when a vehicle caught her attention. The white 4X4 was tearing down the street, heading straight for her. Sunlight reflected off the windshield. The driver wasn't slowing down.

He was going to hit her.

Noelle's heart leapt into her throat. She bent at the knees and launched herself into the air to get out of the truck's way. Pain exploded along her side as she slammed into the concrete. The breath fled her lungs. Noelle didn't stop. She rolled until her body collided with the curb.

The tires of the truck whizzed past her. Horns blared and someone shouted. Noelle shoved into a sitting position and watched in shock as the vehicle took a right turn. It disappeared.

David ran up beside her. Concern was etched across his handsome features. "Don't move. EMS is on the way."

Noelle's mind snapped into law enforcement mode. She

tested each of her limbs and found they were all working. Her coat was dusty from rolling on the street, but the plushy fabric had protected her arms and chest from injury. "I'm okay. Help me up."

David took her proffered hand and placed another on her elbow. His grip was firm but gentle. The warmth of his skin against her palm sent a jolt of awareness through her. Noelle lifted her gaze to his face. His features were both familiar and foreign. The slant of his nose and the curve of his lips were unchanged, but there was a rugged masculinity to the angle of his jaw. A faint scar creased his left cheekbone. That was new. She had the ridiculous urge to reach up and trace it with her finger.

David peered down at her, his brows creased over russet-colored eyes. "You look dazed, Noelle. Did you hit your head?"

No, but it would explain the absurd turn of her thoughts. She had a near-death experience and, instead of focusing on the accident, was fixated on the lawman still holding her hand.

The scent of his aftershave—something earthy and warm—drew her closer. Or maybe that was the memory of their teenage romance. Noelle leaned her head against his chest. That too was both familiar and foreign. Broader, stronger, but with the same comforting feel.

She let out a shuddering breath as the full impact of what could've happened rolled through her. "You saved my life. I heard you call my name. If you hadn't..." Noelle would've been crushed by the truck's tires. "He picked up speed when I saw him. The driver was aiming to kill me."

David wrapped his arms around her, pulling her closer. "I know."

"This isn't over, is it?"

"I'm afraid not. You're in danger, Noelle."

He didn't need to explain why. She'd already figured it out. Margaret's killer had failed to murder Noelle at the nursery. She was a witness.

One the criminal was determined to eliminate.

Two hours later, Noelle nursed a cup of coffee inside the Cutler Police Department. The caffeine wouldn't slow her heart rate down or settle her nerves, but she couldn't bring herself to care. Phones rang throughout the bull pen. A large Christmas tree, sparkling with lights, sat in the corner. Dancing snowflakes decorated the large windows overlooking Main Street. Garland stretched around desks and poinsettias were everywhere.

Noelle sipped her coffee from the safety of the conference room, letting the warmth of the dark brew erase the fear stuck in her core. "Why does it look like Christmas exploded all over the station?"

David chuckled as he glanced up from the paperwork he was reading. They'd been reviewing all the evidence and interviews from Margaret's case. "That's Holly's doing. She's the chief's wife."

As if his words had called him, Chief Aiden James strolled into the conference room. He was tall with dark hair and pleasant features. His mouth was drawn into a hard line.

Noelle's heart sank. "You didn't catch him, did you?"

"No. The truck was recovered about five blocks from the accident. Stolen. The crime scene technicians checked for prints, but the perpetrator wore gloves. We pulled security footage from several stores on Main Street, but none of them are clear enough to identify the driver." Aiden blew out a breath and planted his hands on his hips. "I spoke with Waylon Jennings. He claims to have been at home, asleep, at the time of the accident. Of course, there's no way to be certain that's true."

No. There wasn't. Noelle's hand tightened around the takeaway mug of coffee, slightly crumpling it. "Waylon could've followed us after we interviewed him."

"Did anything about Waylon strike you as familiar?"

"No, but again, I didn't get a good look at the attacker. Waylon is the right height and approximate weight. He has a history of violent behavior, and admitted himself that his marriage to Margaret was rocky." She let out a breath. "Although I can't figure why he would kill Margaret now. Their divorce has been final for almost a year."

"Rage can build over time," David pointed out. "Whoever killed Margaret planned it out." He rose and walked over to the whiteboard, pointing at the farm road running alongside the nursery. "The murderer snuck on to the property. The evidence suggests he brought his own weapon. Samson's Nursery closes at five and business, according to the sales reports of the last few weeks, slows down significantly after three in the afternoon. The killer didn't expect anyone to be there except Margaret."

"I heard voices." Noelle frowned, trying to pull the nugget from her memory banks. "They didn't sound heated.

In fact, I thought Margaret was helping a customer. Whoever killed her was someone she knew and wasn't scared of." She tugged a report closer to her. "Chief, you spoke to Margaret's sister and brother-in-law. Kylie and Brian claimed they weren't working at the nursery that night because Kylie got a migraine. Brian drove her home. Is there any indication there's bad blood in the family?"

Aiden's brows arched. "You think they killed Margaret?"

"It's possible. Kylie inherits the entire business, along with her sister's house and a significant life insurance policy." Noelle lifted the financial document from the table. "Samson's Nursery isn't making a lot of money. In fact, they've borrowed a large sum from a family friend recently. With the assets Kylie has inherited now that her sister is dead, she can pay off the loan and have money left over for a nice nest egg. So, I'll ask again, was there any indication in your interview that things between the sisters were strained?"

He was quiet for a long moment. "It's hard to say. Both Kylie and her husband said Waylon was the only person they could think of who had a grudge against Margaret. They were so distraught over the murder, there wasn't time to press them about anything further." His attention was fixed on the floor, but his gaze was distant, as if Aiden was replaying the conversation in his mind. "I didn't get the sense they were faking their grief however."

Maybe she was heading in the wrong direction, but Noelle didn't like to leave any loose threads. Attention to detail, and pursuing every lead, could make the difference. "I want to talk to their friend, Larry Paulson. The one the

Samsons borrowed money from. He may have some insight into the family."

David hooked his thumbs into the pockets of his pants. "Given what happened this afternoon, it's better for you to take a step back from the investigation."

"No." Her tone was firm. "I won't let this criminal scare me away from this case. Whoever Margaret's killer is, he needs to be arrested and put in prison. I intended to make that happen." Resolve straightened her spine. "The sooner, the better." Noelle glanced at the chief. "Provided you have no objection. This is your jurisdiction, after all."

She held her breath as Aiden's gaze locked on hers. She felt the quiet weight of his assessment. Then he nodded. "Stick close to David. Work the case together. I don't want the killer to catch you alone." Aiden swung his attention toward his officer. "Keep me updated. I'll continue to work additional leads from here."

David nodded. "Understood."

Aiden left the room. The door clicked close behind him, and the silence stretched out.

Noelle could feel David's disapproval from across the room, but he hadn't argued with her right to continue working the case. He'd never been intimidated by her bravery or independence, and although he was protective, it wasn't overbearing. Noelle had forgotten how nice it felt.

He breathed out. "I don't want you to get hurt."

She moved closer to him. "I'll be careful, David. Promise." Noelle's lips lifted in a slight smile. "Besides, I have you watching my back. No one will get close."

"He got close today." A muscle in David's jaw worked.

His gaze swung to hers, fierce and glowering. "You could've died. Leave town, Noelle. It's the smartest thing to do."

"Can you guarantee the killer won't follow me?" She waited for David to work through the logic on his own before continuing, "I'm an FBI agent. Chances are, the killer knows that. He tried to run me down anyway. Going to Memphis won't prevent him from coming after me." She placed a hand on David's arm. The muscles were tense under her palm. "The only way to ensure my safety is to put him behind bars. Let's finish what we started."

SIX

Larry Paulson owned and operated a photography business nestled between a nail salon and a laundromat. Bells hung over the door jangled as David followed Noelle inside. Pictures were artfully displayed on the walls. As was typical for a small-town photographer, Larry specialized in capturing every significant moment in a person's life—from baby photos to eightieth birthday parties and everything in between.

"Sorry, I'm closed." Larry didn't look up from the computer screen he was studying. He was average height with a mop of blond hair and wire-rim glasses. David had met the man a time or two in passing at various functions, but didn't know him well. He vaguely remembered Larry had taken over the shop when the previous owner retired.

Today, the man eluded sadness. His eyes, behind the glasses, were red-rimmed and puffy. As David stepped closer to the counter, he noticed Margaret's photograph on the computer screen. "Excuse me, Larry. I'm sorry to bother you, but we need to ask some questions."

Larry glanced up, seemingly registering his guests for the first time. His eyes widened. With shock? Or fear? David couldn't tell, but he didn't like the way Larry's gaze shot straight to Noelle. Something flickered in the depths of the other man's eyes. It sent David's intuition humming. His fists clenched as he fought the urge to pull Noelle out the door.

Breathe. He reminded himself that Noelle was a trained law enforcement officer. It did little to ease the protective drive surging through his veins. David had worked with women before, many times, but no one inspired these kinds of feelings. *That* wasn't something he wanted to think about either.

Noelle introduced herself and then gestured to the computer screen. "You and Margaret were close?"

"Our mothers were best friends. Margaret and I aren't blood related, but we're practically cousins." He sniffed, tears filming his eyes. "I'm preparing a slide show of photographs for her funeral."

"I'm sorry for your loss." Noelle's tone was comforting and genuine.

"Thank you." Larry swiped under his nose with a tissue and tossed it in a nearby trash can before focusing back on her. A weak smile played on his thin lips. "How can I help you?"

"We're working on piecing together the last days of Margaret's life. It'll help us narrow down what happened to her. Any information you could provide would be helpful. Did Margaret seem worried about anything lately? Stressed in any way?"

Larry picked up a pen from the counter and fiddled

with it. A stall tactic? Perhaps. David had the sense Larry was weighing his words carefully. People rarely liked to speak ill of the dead or cast aspirations on others.

The silence drew out. David let it, and so did Noelle. Sometimes people blurted out crucial information to avoid awkward moments.

Finally, Larry sighed. "Margaret has…" He caught himself. "Had been struggling financially for some time. The nursery isn't doing well. I lent Margaret and Kylie some money a while back and they haven't been able to make the payments. It's caused tension."

"Between you and Margaret? Or between Margaret and her sister?"

"All around. Kylie is a spender. It's part of the reason the business landed in trouble." His nose wrinkled as if he'd smelled something foul. "Her husband is no help. He supposedly works at the nursery, but I've never seen him do an honest day's labor in my life."

"What was Margaret's relationship like with her brother-in-law?"

"They didn't like each other, but they got on for Kylie's sake. Margaret adored her baby sister. There's only a year between them and they were very close." He tilted his head. "What does all this have to do with the murder?"

"We're just trying to understand more about Margaret's life." Noelle gave him a disarming smile. "We heard Margaret was having trouble with her ex-husband."

"Waylon. Yeah, he's a piece of work." Larry crossed his arms over his chest. "He was furious when she got the house in the divorce, but Margaret put up most of the money for the down payment. She was also the only one paying the mortgage. Waylon never contributed. Margaret deserved to get the house."

There was a note of something akin to love buried in Larry's voice. But what kind? The type reserved for a close friend? David didn't get that impression. He decided to press more on that point. "I found it strange that Margaret and Waylon married in the first place. They seem like opposites."

"They were. Margaret..." His gaze drifted to the photograph on the computer screen. In it, Margaret was holding a plant, gazing at the photographer with affection, a laugh playing on her lips. Larry blinked rapidly, as if holding back a fresh wave of tears. "She was something special."

Yep. He'd been in love with her. It added a new layer to an already complicated case, although David didn't know if or how it was relevant. Still, he tucked the information away in the back of his mind. "It was nice of you to loan Margaret the money to keep her business afloat."

Larry tore his gaze away from the computer screen. "What? Oh, the loan. Yeah, well, I didn't have much of a choice. Kylie had run the business into the ground. I didn't want Margaret to lose everything she'd worked for because her sister was irresponsible."

"Must've upset you when Margaret couldn't make the loan payments."

"I was never angry with her." His mouth pursed. "Kylie is a different matter. Of course, now that Margaret is gone, I'll probably never see a dime of my money." His shoulders sagged. "Not that it matters. All things considered, I'd pay double to have Margaret back. Who on earth would've murdered her? She was the kindest—"

His body trembled with barely controlled sobs. Larry muttered something that sounded akin to excuse me and bolted for the rear of the store. His grief was palpable. David found himself second-guessing his first impressions of the man. Larry certainly hadn't said one bad word about Margaret. It seemed he didn't have a reason to kill her.

Noelle pinched the bridge of her nose. "We need to speak to Kylie and her husband."

"Let's go." David took out a business card and scrawled a brief message on the back, requesting Larry to contact him if he thought of anything else that might help the case. Then he escorted Noelle back into the sunshine.

His gaze swept their immediate surroundings. After the close encounter this morning, David wouldn't let his guard down for a moment. Nothing appeared out of the ordinary. Still, he quickly hustled Noelle to his SUV. Once they were on the road, he kept one eye on the rearview mirror.

Just in case they were followed.

"Questioning Kylie is going to take some finesse." Noelle twirled a strand of hair between her fingers. "We don't have any evidence either she or her husband are responsible for Margaret's murder."

"Agreed. We need to tread lightly." David didn't want to traumatize the family further. Everyone he'd spoken to had been clear that Kylie and Margaret had been close. "It's my understanding Kylie and her husband are working at the nursery today. They elected to keep it open."

Noelle's eyes brightened. "That works perfectly. We can question them without it being formal or awkward."

"How do you intend to do that?"

She tossed him a grin. "Granny still needs a Christmas tree."

SEVEN

Kylie Samson Turner was a curvy woman with a dark haircut into a face-framing bob. She wore an apron with the Samson's Nursery logo embroidered on the front over her casual clothes. Her husband, Brian, was bald and fit. His work gloves were covered in sap from hauling Christmas trees for customers. Both of them had shadows under their eyes.

Noelle's heart pinched tight, and she second-guessed her suspicion that either of them had something to do with Margaret's death. Their grief was visible. But five years as an FBI agent had taught her that sometimes the most sinister criminals could successfully fake innocence.

"We have to keep the nursery up and running to pay the bills." Kylie's posture was slumped. She leaned against her husband, who wrapped an arm over her shoulders. "The town has been incredibly supportive. People have come by to bring food, give their condolences, and make a purchase to help us get through this difficult time."

That was nice. Even as a teen, Noelle had always

admired the way Cutler residents banded together when something tragic happened in the community. It was so different from living in the city. She didn't even know her neighbors' names.

"Have you made any progress on figuring out who killed Margaret?" Brian asked.

"We're still tracking down leads." David pulled a notepad out of the front pocket of his uniform. "It would help if you could answer a few questions for us."

Kylie stiffened, and a tear leaked from her eye. She swiped at it with jerky movements. "I can't. Talking about it upsets me and there are customers here. We'll have to do it another time."

Strange. Normally, the family wanted to find the killer as much—if not more—than the police did. Noelle's initial suspicion about Kylie grew. Did she have something to do with her sister's death? Was that part of the reason she was so distraught?

Or was she telling the truth and unable to answer questions because the grief was too overwhelming?

It was time to fall back on Plan B. There was more than one way to question Kylie. Noelle offered the older woman a sympathetic look. "I know this must be incredibly difficult for you. We can speak another time. Would you mind helping me select a Christmas tree for my grandmother? She needs something fluffy, but not too tall."

"Sure." Kylie let out a breath, the tension leaving her spine. "Come this way."

Noelle glanced at David, and their eyes met for a moment. He gave a slight nod, nearly imperceptible, except she'd been watching for it. David would question Brian while Noelle would see what information she could get out of Kylie.

The scent of evergreen wrapped its embrace around Noelle as she followed Kylie to the Christmas tree section. Her heart skipped a beat. She glanced over her shoulder, the feeling of being watched making the hair on the back of her neck stand on end. A few customers meandered around the property. No one seemed to pay them any attention.

Maybe it was just being back here. Noelle didn't think she'd ever be able to pick out a Christmas tree again without remembering Margaret and the attack.

"Your store is lovely." Noelle forced herself to focus on the task at hand. "Do you have a lot of business at Christmas time?"

"A fair amount, although things are quiet in January and February. No one wants to work in their yard during the cold months." Kylie stopped in front of several trees. "These are what you're looking for. Not too tall, but full."

Noelle considered the selections while mulling over the best way to get Kylie to talk. She decided empathy was the way to go. "I'm sorry about your sister. I have a brother who lives in New York. We're close and the idea of losing him... it's devastating."

"Thank you." Kylie's voice was low. Her chin trembled. "I appreciate all you're doing to catch Margaret's killer. I told Chief James that it must've been a robbery or something like that. It doesn't make sense for anyone to have targeted Margaret."

A robbery wasn't likely. The register at the front counter hadn't been touched, and Margaret had been speaking with her killer. Noelle tilted her head. "What about Waylon?"

"Waylon was a nightmare as a husband—a drunk and a cheater—but he was strangely protective of my sister. To my knowledge, he never laid a hand on her."

"What was Margaret's relationship like with Larry Paulson?"

"Larry?" Kylie rocked back on her heels and her eyes widened with surprise. "You spoke to Larry?"

"He was a close friend of your sister's. Larry didn't have many nice things to say about Waylon."

Kylie's nose wrinkled. "I'm sure Larry didn't have nice things to say about me or my husband either. He's not fond of us. Larry believes we took advantage of Margaret..." She grew quiet for several heartbeats. "Maybe we did. Margaret loved working here. Plants were a passion for her, and when we inherited the business from our parents, it made sense to continue working together. But this place has never been anything more than a job to me. A way to earn income."

"Did that cause an issue between you and your sister?"

"No. Margaret understood my point of view. She was happy to handle most of the business aspects."

"Still, it can't have been easy. Especially during the lean months. Larry explained he loaned money to keep the nursery afloat and that it caused friction between all of you."

Kylie licked her lips. "It did. I wanted Margaret to sell the business. On paper, things looked good, and we had potential buyers who'd made offers. She refused. Instead, Margaret went behind my back and borrowed money from Larry."

Noelle kept her expression placid. "That must've been difficult for you. If my sister did that, I'd be pretty angry with her."

Kylie's chin trembled and fresh tears welled in her eyes. "I was. We didn't speak for months. Things had finally thawed out between us..."

The rest of her sentence hung in the air.

And then she was murdered.

"I'm so sorry." Noelle's heart squeezed tight at the look of devastation on the other woman's face. It was obvious Kylie was carrying around a great deal of regret. "What will you do now? Will you sell the business?"

"I don't know. I can't think that far ahead." Kylie took a shuddering breath. "Which tree would you like?"

Noelle selected one. She'd sensed the conversation with Kylie was over, and although Noelle wanted to push for more information, experience held her back. She didn't want to risk Kylie would realize she was a suspect and lawyer up. It was much better to have her communicating with the police.

Kylie tore a tag off the tree and handed it to her. "Take this to the register. I'll have Brian deliver the tree to your vehicle."

"Thank you." Noelle followed the path to the front counter. The register was manned by a teenager who efficiently rang her up. David and Brian were already tying the Christmas tree to the roof of the SUV by the time Noelle went to the parking lot.

She did her level best to ignore the muscles rippling underneath David's uniform, but failed miserably. And when he offered his hand to assist Noelle into the passenger seat, butterflies fluttered in her stomach.

Storm clouds gathered in the distance as they hit the road. A metaphor for Noelle's relationship with David. She was heading into dangerous territory. This spark of attraction had nowhere to go. She lived in Memphis. His life was in Cutler. Friendship was all they could have.

Besides, it was asinine to feel this much pull toward a man she hadn't seen in nearly ten years. A lot had changed in that time. David was practically a stranger now. She needed to keep her head on straight and focus on the case.

Decision made, she turned toward David. "Did you learn anything new from Brian?"

"Nope. He was tight-lipped. I got the sense he's hiding something, but I can't pinpoint what. Did you have any luck with Kylie?"

"I did. She admitted things were tense between her and Margaret." Noelle summarized her conversation with Kylie. "I believe her grief is real, but I can't mark her off the suspect list yet. Kylie benefits from Margaret's death the most. She inherits everything, including the business. Now they can sell it, which is what Kylie wanted to do in the first place."

"Except she's not the one who attacked you. A man did."

"Brian and Kylie are each other's alibis. Who's to say they aren't lying? It wouldn't be the first time a husband and wife teamed up to commit murder."

David's mouth flattened. "It's also possible Kylie doesn't know her husband is responsible for Margaret's death. She claimed to have taken a sleeping pill and gone to bed. If that's true, he could've snuck out of the house and confronted Margaret, then killed her."

Noelle nodded, frustration building inside her. "The lack of physical evidence in this case is hampering us."

David's radio crackled and dispatch announced a traffic accident nearby. He glanced at Noelle. "We're close to that. Do you mind waiting in the car while I handle things?"

"Not at all."

He made a right turn. It took over an hour to handle the paperwork for the minor fender bender and get back on the road. Noelle spent the time taking notes about the case on her phone, recording her thoughts and observations. Something was niggling her, but she couldn't figure out what. She needed sleep. And food. Dinnertime was quickly approaching, and she'd skipped lunch.

As they pulled into her grandmother's driveway, David's headlights swept across the side of the house. A man dressed in black bolted from the back door and ran toward the woods bordering the house. An intruder. Noelle's heart jumped in her chest. "David."

"I saw him." David had already killed the engine and shoved his door open. "Check on your grandmother. I'll go after him."

Noelle launched herself out of the vehicle and up the walkway. She pulled her weapon from its holster underneath her jacket. Nerves jittered her stomach, making her nauseated. She swallowed back the bile. A part of her wanted to race inside, another part was terrified of what she would find. Her fingers trembled as she opened the front door.

The house was silent. The familiar scent of baking

bread and pot roast wafted over her. Noelle's pulse picked up speed. She drew in deep breaths to counteract the adrenaline coursing through her. "Granny?"

No answer. Noelle pushed the door open farther with her foot and crossed the threshold, embedded training causing her to use caution when all she wanted to do was burst into the house. But she couldn't assume there was only one intruder. Noelle was no help to her grandmother dead.

The foyer was empty, the house quiet. Prayers in her heart, Noelle continued forward, gun leading the way. "Granny, answer me."

EIGHT

A branch smacked David in the face as he barreled through the woods after the suspect. The man was nothing more than a darker shadow against the foliage. Dusk was encroaching by the second, along with another thunderstorm, which limited visibility. Sweat beaded between his shoulder blades and his breath quickened. David fired more energy into his legs. He couldn't let the man get away.

The crack of a gun broke through the air and something whizzed past David, slamming into a nearby tree trunk.

The perpetrator was shooting at him.

David dove to the ground as another shot ripped through the night. Fury fueled his adrenaline as he rolled to take shelter behind an ancient oak tree. He came up on one knee, his gun held between two hands for stabilization. He peered around the bark into the woods. "Police! Drop your weapon and put your hands behind your head!"

Another bullet collided with the oak tree, spraying bark and wood chips. David gritted his teeth. His heart beat rapidly, and he took a deep breath to slow the pace. The thunderous roar in his ears reduced as he focused his senses on the woods beyond his vision. The shooter was on his left. Not moving.

What was he waiting for?

Maybe he thought David was dead. Or he was calculating his next move.

Sirens blared. Backup was on the way. Noelle must've called them because David hadn't had time. He rose from his crouch and peered around the tree once more, but the darkness hid the perpetrator. Nightfall made it impossible to see beyond his own immediate surroundings.

Frustration revved inside him. As much as he hated to admit it, David needed to get out of there. He was a sitting duck without anyone to watch his back. It hadn't been smart to pursue the intruder on his own to begin with, evidenced by the fact that he'd almost been shot. Aiden would have his hide.

Silently, David eased away from the oak tree and headed back toward Noelle's house. As he broke free of the tree line, she ran across the yard, her curly hair flying behind her. The motion detection lights on the house illuminated the stark fear in her expression. Panic alighted in his heart. David increased his speed and met her halfway. She launched herself into his arms.

He embraced her back but wasn't able to relish the way her body fit so perfectly with his. Concern kept all of that at bay. "Your grandmother?"

"She's fine. Granny locked herself in the bathroom when the intruder broke in." Noelle backed away and scanned his body. "I heard shots and thought…"

The cause for her distress immediately became clear.

Him. She'd been worried about him.

Something inside David twisted hard. It was illogical and irrational, but there was a connection between them that defied reason. Memories whispered through him. Year after year of shared childhood experiences. At one time, Noelle had been his best friend. The smart and brave girl he'd once known had become a beautiful and caring woman. The kind of woman who could melt all his defenses and steal his heart.

"I'm okay." He glanced behind him at the woods, then wrapped an arm around her waist. "Come on. Let's get you inside."

Aiden arrived and took their statements. The intruder hadn't taken anything from the house, including Sheila's purse, which was sitting on the kitchen counter in plain view. The timing of the break-in couldn't be a coincidence.

David leaned against the island. "The shooter was after Noelle."

"Certainly looks like it." Aiden glanced into the living room. Noelle and her grandmother were sitting on the couch, holding hands and talking. "He didn't attempt to hurt Sheila, thank God. It was smart to lock herself in the bathroom."

David nodded and then frowned. "None of this makes sense. Margaret was stabbed. If the killer owned a gun, why didn't he just shoot her?"

"Because he didn't intend to kill Margaret when he went to the nursery." Aiden scraped a hand through his mop of dark hair, making it stand on end. "I got the preliminary autopsy report. The coroner believes Margaret was stabbed with scissors, and Kylie confirmed that a set is missing from the front desk."

"A spontaneous act of rage? I don't know if I completely buy that. Otherwise, why wasn't his vehicle in the parking lot?"

"That's a good question. The only thing I can think of is that the killer didn't want anyone to know he was there."

David mulled that over. Strange. He didn't know how that fit with what they already knew about the case. "Okay, let's run with that. The killer and Margaret are meeting in secret for some reason. While together, they get into an argument. The killer grabs the scissors from the front desk, follows her deeper into the store, and then stabs her in anger."

"Sounds about right." Aiden rubbed his jaw. "Then he realizes Noelle is there. He panics, worried that she's seen or heard something that can identify him. Then he attacks and attempts to kill her." He drops his hand, his gaze turning hard. "And when that fails, he tries again and again."

David's own anger mirrored his boss's. Noelle didn't deserve to be hunted down by a killer intent on silencing her. Whoever this man was, they had to stop him.

"It sounds like a lover's quarrel gone wrong," David noted.

"Agreed. Which brings us back to Waylon." Aiden settled his cowboy hat on his head. "I'm going to question him again. Let's see if he has an alibi for this evening."

"Talk to Larry Paulson too. I got the sense he was in love with Margaret. Maybe she didn't return his affection."

"Will do." Aiden headed for the front door and then

paused. "One more thing. Holly's arranging a holiday party at our house." A smile played on his lips. "My wife insists that crime fighting can wait for two hours while we celebrate together. Chase and Faith will be there with their kids. Bring Noelle along. It's tomorrow afternoon after church."

Despite the seriousness of the murder investigation, David's heart lightened at the thought of a party. Holly, a social worker, was good at reminding them to stop and give thanks. Another member of their small staff, Chase McKenzie, and his wife, Faith, were returning from a family vacation. It would be nice to see them and talk about something other than killers and threats.

He nodded. "I'll be there for sure and I'll invite Noelle too."

"Good. Call me if you need anything." Aiden opened the door. "I'll be in touch."

David locked the door behind his boss. Then he turned into the living room. Sheila and Noelle both looked up at him. Decades separated the women, but they shared the same set of resolve in their jaws and tilt to their heads. He sensed they were in the middle of an argument.

Sheila huffed. "David, explain to my granddaughter that she is not leaving this house and heading back to Memphis."

His gaze locked on Noelle. Heat rose in her cheeks. "I'm worried about Granny's safety. It didn't occur to me that the killer might break into her house and threaten her."

"He didn't threaten me. *I'm* not the one he was looking for, and I don't want you carting yourself off to Memphis with a killer on your tail. I know you're tough, Noelle, but you can't face this all alone. Here you have David and the entire police department looking out for you." Sheila's eyes pleaded with David. "Tell her."

"As much as I hate to get in the middle of an argument between you two, I admit I'm with Sheila on this." Noelle opened her mouth to argue, and he lifted a hand to ward her off. "How about I stay the night in the guest bedroom? Then we can make a plan tomorrow morning on how to handle things. Patrol officers can do frequent trips through the neighborhood to monitor the house. Or Sheila can stay with a friend during the day, if we're gone."

"Those are excellent suggestions. Problem solved." Sheila beamed and rose. "I'm going into the kitchen to warm up dinner, which I'm sure has gone stone cold by now. Then we can decorate the beautiful tree y'all brought." She squinted at Noelle and David. "I don't want any more talk about the case tonight. We need a break from murders and mayhem. Some holiday cheer is just the ticket."

Noelle's shoulders dropped. "Yes, ma'am."

David nodded to show he agreed.

Sheila bustled out of the room. Moments later, holiday music poured from the kitchen followed by the sounds of pots and pans banging on the stove.

Noelle rose from the couch and glared at him. "Traitor. You're supposed to be on my side."

The words were harsh, but there was no heat behind them. David lightly grabbed her wrist and tugged Noelle into his arms. She hugged him back, wrapping her slender arms around his waist. Her head rested on his chest and he brushed a light kiss against the crown of her hair. The strands smelled like apples and cinnamon. He breathed it in, letting the moment wash away the last of his tension.

"I am on your side, Noelle. Sheila's right. Here you have the entire police force, and me, watching out for you." He squeezed her gently. "And if I'm being completely honest, I'm not ready to see you go."

She sighed. "I have to go at some point, though, David. My life isn't here."

"I know." The attraction and connection between them had nowhere to go beyond friendship. Getting in deeper with Noelle was a mistake, but David couldn't stop himself. He'd likely end up heartbroken, but his love life was already littered with a string of regrets. What was one more?

Deep down, in his core, David believed it was far better to have loved and lost than never having tried at all.

His gaze went to the window and the darkness beyond the well-lit yard. Was the killer out there? Watching? David held Noelle closer and sent up a prayer.

Please, God, help me keep her safe.

NINE

Noelle lifted her voice skyward, the Christmas hymn bathing her in tranquility. The church pews were packed with worshipers. Sunshine streamed through the glass-stained windows casting rainbows over the altar. To her left, Sheila twirled the strand of pearls around her neck as she sang. David, on Noelle's right, tilted the hymn book so she could read the words.

A sense of peace and rightness washed over her. It was a welcome relief. The attack last night had shaken her. Badly. She'd accepted the risk associated with her job a long time ago, but for the killer to have invaded her grandmother's home... that was something altogether different. The church service was a reminder that God was watching over them. She was grateful for His protection.

Noelle peeked at David out of the corner of her eye. Today, he was off duty and the maroon shirt was the perfect backdrop for his dark hair and chiseled features. Her heart skipped a beat. It was an involuntary reaction Noelle couldn't control, even if she wanted to. Decorating the

Christmas tree last night, drinking hot chocolate, and telling old stories until nearly midnight had melted the last of her resistance. David had morphed from the fun-loving teenager she'd once known into a mature and thoughtful man. Her attraction to him was growing in leaps and bounds with every second spent in his presence.

It was a complication she didn't need.

Her life was in Memphis. Her job. Being around David was wonderful, but it wasn't permanent. Mentally, she understood that, but her heart refused to get the message. David made her yearn for things she hadn't thought about in a long time. Marriage and a family. A home.

It was a confusing, jumbled mess and not something Noelle could think about now. Not when a killer had her in his sights.

The church service ended, and everyone traipsed outside. The air was frosty. Noelle zipped up her jacket and arranged her scarf around her neck. "Granny, are you going to be okay this afternoon? I can stay with you—"

"Nonsense." Sheila waved at a group of older ladies standing off to the side. "I'm going to have lunch with my friends and then go to Linda's house after. She needs help to address her Christmas cards. This cold weather really upsets her arthritis."

"We shouldn't be long." Noelle and David needed to interview Larry, and then they were attending the Christmas party. She didn't feel quite right about leaving her grandmother, especially after yesterday's attack. "A few hours at most."

"Take all the time you need." Sheila patted Noelle's arm. "I'll be fine, dear."

Then she turned to David and wagged her finger. "Take good care of my granddaughter, young man."

"I will, ma'am."

Sheila shot him a smile wide enough to deepen the crow's feet at the corners of her eyes and then shot down the sidewalk to join her friends. The gaggle of women moved together toward the diner on the corner.

Noelle watched her grandmother go with a mix of affection and envy. Outside of family, she didn't have two people in her contact list to call when hard times came. Would she ever have that sense of community that came so easily to her granny?

David placed a hand on the small of Noelle's back, interrupting the train of her thoughts. "Ready to go? Larry said he'll be at his studio for the next hour or so this morning. I don't want to miss him."

"Yes. Let's go." Noelle fell into step beside him. It was impossible to feel the warmth of David's palm through the thick layer of her jacket and sweater, but the pressure was enough to quicken her heartbeat.

The walk to Larry's studio was a short one. David held the door open for Noelle. As she crossed the threshold, the invisible armor worn for interviewing suspects slipped over her emotions, shielding them.

Larry was once again stationed behind the counter, working on the computer. He rose when they entered. "Noelle. David. You have good timing. I was heading home in fifteen minutes." He lifted his wire-rim glasses and rubbed his eyes. "I haven't been sleeping much lately, as you can imagine. I've fallen behind in my work, which is the only reason I'm here on a Sunday morning."

"Thanks for taking the time to speak to us." Noelle rested her arms on the front counter. "We won't keep you long."

She glanced at David, and he nodded slightly to show she should take the lead in questioning Larry. She focused back on the photographer. "I'm not sure if you're aware, but citizens offered information about Margaret to the police. We received a tip about you. Apparently, you and Margaret had an argument three days before her murder. A very public and heated argument."

Larry's mouth flattened into a thin line. "That has nothing to do with her murder."

"Maybe not, but it's our job to determine that, not yours." Noelle kept her tone calm but firm. "What was the argument about?"

He hesitated and then said, "Someone at the nursery is stealing. Embezzling actually."

Shock vibrated through Noelle. From the way David stiffened slightly, he was just as surprised. He leaned on the counter. "How do you know?"

"As part of the loan agreement, I may review the nursery's financial records. I discovered invoices made out to fake companies. Someone was removing money from the corporate account under the guise of paying vendors."

Noelle's mind whirled with the new information. There were only three potential people who could've faked those invoices: Margaret, her sister, Kylie, or Kylie's husband. And one of them was dead. Had Kylie or her husband killed Margaret to hide the fact that they were embezzling money? It was entirely possible.

Frustration bled into Noelle's voice. "You didn't think

this information was important for us to know?" She hit the desk with her palm. "We asked if there was any reason someone might have wanted Margaret dead and you purposefully held this back."

"Because Kylie is my family." Larry roared the sentence as if he was a wounded bear. He took several deep breaths and when he spoke again, his tone was more respectful. "Listen to me. Kylie would never hurt her sister. Never. I don't know what happened with the fake invoices. Margaret went through a rough time financially. Making the mortgage payments on the house and paying for the divorce attorney had drained her savings. I'm unclear about who was actually embezzling from the corporate accounts."

"What did Margaret say when you confronted her?"

"She pretended to be ignorant." He blew out a breath. "But I know—" Larry caught himself and shook his head. "I knew her. She was aware of the embezzlement. The conversation got heated when I demanded that she admit it. Margaret refused."

"Is it possible she was covering for her sister?"

"I don't know." Larry looked broken, his shoulders sagging inward and his gaze down. "Maybe. Or Brian. Margaret would've done anything to protect Kylie, even hide the fact that her husband was stealing money. Or, like I said, Margaret was the one embezzling. This information may have nothing to do with her murder. In fact, I'm almost certain it doesn't. Brian and Kylie loved Margaret dearly. They wouldn't have killed her."

The last words came out in a whisper, as if Larry was trying to convince himself. Sympathy erased Noelle's earlier frustration. It was clear Larry was hurting and hadn't wanted to accuse his close family friend of murdering her own sister. Still, Noelle wished he'd offered this information earlier.

David and Noelle questioned Larry further, but he had nothing more to add. He agreed to send them the financial information proving the embezzlement. They stepped back outside into the cold.

Noelle tucked her hands in her pockets. "What do you think?"

David grimaced. "I think we need to speak to Brian and Kylie again."

"Agreed, but it would be better if we had some additional evidence before we do. I'd like to search Margaret's house. Maybe she kept a journal or notes about what was going on at the nursery. Or we'll find evidence that she was the one embezzling the money."

"Good thinking. We can do it this afternoon. I'm not supposed to talk shop at the holiday party today, but I'll find five minutes to pull Aiden aside and update him on what's going on."

Twenty minutes later, Noelle was trying not to suppress her nerves as she was pulled into a house full of people by Aiden's wife. Holly was a cute blond with a bubbly personality. She wore an oversized sweater with dancing Santa on it and dangly ornament earrings. Like the police station, the house was covered in holiday decor.

Noelle's eyes widened as the Christmas tree in the living room came into view. "Wow. I don't think I've ever seen so many ornaments on one tree."

Holly laughed and blushed. "I know. I go overboard. Christmas is my favorite holiday." She pulled Noelle closer to a young woman on the ground with a toddler. "This is my friend, Faith, and her daughter, Anna. Faith's husband, Chase, is that handsome man over there holding their little boy."

David followed the women into the living room. He shook Chase's hand warmly and eyed the infant with interest. "I can't believe how big Hudson has gotten. What are you feeding him?"

Chase chuckled. "Milk, same as any other baby. But this kid eats often, and you'd watch out if you don't have it ready when he's hungry. Hudson has a temper and will let you know it." He tilted his head at Noelle. "Nice to meet you."

"Likewise."

Noelle barely got the word out before Holly was introducing her to the next people. The steady stream of conversation, the homey atmosphere, and the delicious food was the perfect way to spend the afternoon. David caught up to her in the kitchen as Noelle was placing dirty plates in the dishwasher.

"Are you okay? Holly didn't overwhelm you, did she?"

"Not at all. She made me feel right at home." Noelle wiped her hands on a dish towel. "Your friends are amazing, David. You've got something really special here."

His gaze warmed. "Yeah. I do."

"Noelle Logan, you aren't doing my dishes, are you?" Holly bustled into the kitchen with a stack of plates in her arms. "You're my guest."

"I'm happy to help." Noelle took the dishware from the other woman and set them in the sink. "Everything was fabulous. Thank you so much for inviting me."

Holly beamed. "You're welcome. I hope this won't be

the only time we see you. I'd love for you to come back whenever you visit your grandmother." She turned to leave the kitchen and then looked over her shoulder, a teasing smile playing on her lips. "Look up, you two."

Noelle glanced above her head. Mistletoe dangled from the ceiling, right over her and David. Heat immediately infused her cheeks, and her gaze shot to Holly.

The other woman wagged her eyebrows. "Aiden and I are usually the only ones who do dishes in this house."

She deftly left the room, the swinging door drifting shut behind her. The air seemed to be sucked from the room. Noelle didn't dare look David in the eye. "It's just a silly tradition."

He drew closer. Every cell in Noelle's body noticed the tiny sliver of space separating them. The scent of his aftershave teased her senses. Her pulse skittered like a faulty Christmas tree bulb when David cupped her face. His thumb skated across the delicate skin over her cheek as he lifted her chin gently until she was forced to meet his gaze.

Oh, her heart. It couldn't take the longing buried in his russet-colored eyes. The desire. The need. David's focus dropped to her lips. "I'm a traditional guy." He gradually raised his eyes to meet hers again. "Noelle, can I kiss you under the mistletoe?"

Her breath stilled. She should say no. They were catapulting into dangerous territory, heartbreaking territory. But Noelle couldn't force the word past her lips.

Instead, she nodded.

Slowly, ever so slowly, David's mouth inched toward hers. It was achingly sweet, the anticipation, the seconds drawing out until Noelle's entire focus was on the man in front of her. The sounds of the party melted away. Their breath mingled one moment before his lips captured hers.

It was like coming home.

Noelle sank into the kiss, knowing that nothing would ever be the same.

TEN

The next morning, David opened the front door to Margaret Samson's house and flipped on the light in the entryway. Noelle, huddled in her coat against the brisk wind, stood on the front porch. The neighborhood behind her was quiet. Most people were at work, although an elderly gentleman trimmed hedges three houses down. Margaret's property was only half a mile from the nursery. Her sister, Kylie, lived on the next street over.

David stepped aside so Noelle could enter the house ahead of him. The scent of her apple-and-cinnamon shampoo drifted in her wake. It sent every cell in his body humming. The kiss they'd shared last night had unleashed the undercurrent of attraction running between them. A mistake, one he hadn't anticipated until it was too late.

He cared about her. Deeply. More than he wanted to admit. But David was also realistic enough to understand their future was uncertain. Noelle lived in a different state for starters, and even if that weren't true, he didn't have the best track record with romantic relationships.

Dependable David. The moniker beat a drum in his brain last night, making it impossible to sleep. His ex-girlfriend had initially been happy when they started dating, but that had morphed into boredom. Wouldn't Noelle feel the same after several weeks or months? Maybe it was better she didn't live in Cutler. They could share this sweet moment together and then go their separate ways. The memory would be enough.

Or so he told himself.

David's phone vibrated with an incoming text as he shut the front door against the wintery day. He removed his cell from his pocket and scanned the message. "Aiden confirmed with the employees of Barzilla that Waylon was working on the night of Margaret's murder and during the break-in at your grandmother's house. He's not responsible."

Noelle's lips flattened into a thin line. "Good. That removes one suspect from our list. It's more imperative than ever that we narrow down who was embezzling from the nursery."

She tugged on her scarf, unwrapping it from her neck. The cut from the attack on her first night in town became visible. It followed the long column of her neck. David's gut knotted as he remembered just how close she'd come to losing her life.

He tore his gaze away from the wound. "What kind of evidence are you hoping to find?"

"Ideally, I'd like to find a journal or notes about the embezzlement at the nursery," Noelle continued. "Aiden has interviewed several of Margaret's friends. They remarked that she was very organized. If Margaret isn't responsible for the fake invoices—which is the most likely scenario—then she must've looked into the matter after Larry brought it to her attention."

David nodded. It was worth a try. Right now, they had theories and not enough hard evidence. As it stood now, Kylie and her husband could say Margaret was responsible for the embezzlement at the nursery and there was no way to refute that claim.

The house had an open floor plan. The entryway melded into a dining room on the right and the kitchen straight ahead with the living room beyond. Greenhouses were visible in the backyard. A hallway on the left led to the rear bedrooms and the entrance to the garage.

David traversed the hallway and came to a stop in the doorway of the first bedroom. It'd been converted to an office. "Let's start here."

After Margaret's murder, the police department had executed a search warrant on the property. The crime scene technicians had taken Margaret's laptop for analysis and did a cursory glance through the desk, but had found nothing connected to the slaying. That'd happened early in the investigation, however, before David and Noelle had uncovered the embezzlement at the nursery.

Noelle shrugged off her jacket and dropped it in an overstuffed chair near the window. A matching ottoman rested on the carpet and a bookmarked novel sat on the small table nearby. The reading nook was nestled near a wall of shelves weighed down by popular fiction and horticulture textbooks. She ran her fingers over some binders on the bottom shelf. "I'll start here. Why don't you take the desk?"

David circled around the ornate wooden desk. Drawers

with brass handles beckoned. He opened the first one and rummaged through the office supplies. Margaret was incredibly organized. Everything had a place and was meticulously labeled. Sorting through the contents was easy. He closed the last drawer with a sigh. "Nothing of importance here."

Noelle was quiet. She'd perched on the ottoman, a binder open on her lap. Her hair was loose. The gorgeous strands were like a waterfall hiding her exquisite features. She flipped the page in the blinder and made a humming sound.

David came up behind her. "What did you find?"

"Ledgers. They're old, but Margaret has made notes in the margin."

"Paper ledgers? Most businesses use electronic programs to keep track of business income and expenses."

"I suspect these are her own personal backups, used to double-check the accounting system. The ledgers go back as far as her parents' ownership of the nursery." Noelle looked up, excitement brightening her eyes. "I was right. She traced the embezzlement back through the years. And look at this. She notes it all started after Kylie and Brian were married."

David peered over her shoulder at the ledger. Sure enough, Margaret's neat handwriting outlined the timing of the fake invoices. Brian's name was listed with several question marks beside it. He rocked back on his heels. "If Margaret uncovered her brother-in-law was stealing from the company, she might've confronted him in an attempt to protect her sister."

"And it may have led to her death." Noelle snapped the

ledger shut. "Margaret called you on the day of her murder. Maybe this is what she wanted to talk about. We need to pull Brian into the police station for questioning—"

The sound of shattering glass cut her off. Without consciously thinking about it, David grabbed Noelle's arm and pulled her to the carpet. Heat erupted from a blaze along the wall closest to the window, eating up a corner of the old desk like it was a pile of firewood. Smoke began filling the room at a rapid place. Through the busted window, David glimpsed a figure in black racing across the yard.

A Molotov cocktail. Cheap to make, and judging by the scent, filled with gasoline. The perpetrator was attempting to burn down the house with them inside. David's heart rate spiked. "We need to get out of here."

Noelle clutched the ledger to her chest. "He's still out there. The fire may be designed to flush us out in order to shoot us."

It was a terrifying proposition. Still, they couldn't stay in the burning house. David dialed 911 as he directed Noelle toward the doorway leading to the hall. Sweat beaded along his brow. The sound of more glass breaking was followed by whooshes of heat as flames erupted in the living room. They licked the front door, blocking the easiest method for escape.

He backtracked, heading for the master bedroom. Smoke poured from the room. It stung his eyes and clogged his throat. With growing horror, David realized the fire surrounded them.

Noelle gripped his arm, her fingers digging into his skin through the fabric of his uniform. "We're trapped."

ELEVEN

Thick smoke and gasoline flumes choked Noelle. She dropped to her knees in the hallway, still clutching the ledger to her chest. David lowered himself next to her, his voice rapidly spitting out their location to dispatch. Then he hung up the phone. Police and firefighters were on the way, but Cutler was a small town, and it would take time to coordinate a response. It'd be too late to save them under the current circumstances.

David cupped her face. The heat from the flames surrounding them was intense, but it was nothing compared to the fierce determination in his eyes. "We're getting out of here."

"How?" The word came out on a cough. Noelle's gaze swept the immediate area. Heat singed the hair on her arms. Sweat poured down her back. It was incredible how quickly the old house had been eaten by the fire. Just what the killer was counting on.

David grabbed her hand and tugged her down another part of the hallway. "This way. Come on."

She followed close behind him, barely able to see through the smoke. David stopped, reached up and twisted a doorknob, but gestured for her to stay back. He pushed the door open slightly, peered in and then a second later threw it open completely. Her heart wept with joy when she realized where David was leading her.

The garage.

Noelle crawled across the threshold onto the cool cement flooring. The double bay doors were down, blocking them from the killer's view. The only light came from a line of windows along the very top edge of the garage. Whoever had set the house on fire hadn't been able to throw a Molotov cocktail into this space. David slammed the door closed, momentarily shielding them from the heat and flames.

She sagged against a wall and focused on taking deep breaths to clear her lungs from smoke. "Thank you, God." Noelle reached for David's hand again as he took a seat beside her. "You saved us."

"Not yet." His tone was grim. "We could open the garage doors, but I prefer to wait for the first responders to arrive. I don't want to give the killer a chance to shoot us as we're escaping." His gaze went to the shut door they'd just come through. "Still, we may have no choice if the police and firefighters don't arrive soon. Do you have your gun?"

She nodded. Noelle was also still clutching the ledger to her chest. She lowered it to the floor and took more deep breaths. Beside her, David did the same. Both of them clearing the smoke from their lungs and preparing to fight their way out of the burning house if necessary.

Noelle was still holding his hand. She interlocked their

fingers, a sense of peace and trust washing over her. Nothing about this situation was normal. Or safe. But facing it with David by her side made it bearable. He would never let anyone harm her. It was comforting and special and unlike anything she'd ever experienced with another man.

The wail of incoming sirens was like a beacon of hope. Within moments, police and firefighters flooded the area. David and Noelle were treated by EMS, but released with orders to take it easy. Not likely.

They still had a killer to find.

Aiden joined them in the driveway, as firefighters struggled to put the blaze out. His mouth was set in a grim line, ash dotting his uniform and cowboy hat. "Most of the neighbors have gone to work. The old man three doors down saw a figure in black approaching the house before the fire broke out, but he couldn't identify him with any clarity. His eyesight is too poor."

"I didn't get a good look at the arsonist either," David echoed. He gestured to the ledger in Noelle's hand. "We found evidence that indicates Brian is behind the embezzlement at the nursery. It stands to reason, if Margaret confronted him, Brian may have killed her to prevent Kylie from uncovering his secret. I want to interview him."

"That's going to be difficult. I already had an officer drive by the Turners' house to see if they were there. Brian answered the door but refused to voluntarily come down to the station for questioning. He was dressed in street clothing—jeans and a T-shirt—and didn't smell like gasoline."

Noelle shivered in the cold. Her jacket was a casualty of

the fire. "That doesn't mean he didn't set the fire. The Turners live one street over. Brian had plenty of time to return home, change his clothes and clean up."

"I agree with you, but my hands are tied. We don't have enough evidence to arrest him."

She bit back a frustrating urge to kick the nearby tire of an ambulance. Aiden was right. They didn't have enough evidence to arrest Brian. Margaret's notes weren't proof of embezzlement or of murder. Forensics would have to comb through the Turners' finances to uncover purchases that their income couldn't verify, but that would take time. Time they didn't have. The killer was attacking with more frequency. Noelle had narrowly escaped his clutches, but she wasn't under any illusions. He would keep coming for her until she was dead.

Noelle willed her brain to think rationally. "If Brian won't come to the station, then maybe he'll speak to us in his home." She lifted the ledger. "Confronting him with the notes Margaret made could loosen his lips."

The three of them made a plan. Then David and Noelle got into his vehicle and drove the short distance away to the Turners' house. It was a two-story with a small stoop and unhealthy looking bushes in front. Brian was on the driveway, blowing pine needles off the sidewalk. His nose was red from the cold and his bald head bare.

He glowered as they approached. "Come back to hound us some more." He flipped off the blower with an angry jerk as he met them on the road. "Y'all might spend a bit more time looking for Margaret's killer instead of accusing her family of horrible things. We had nothing to do with the murder or any of the other attacks."

Noelle was surprised by the force of Brian's anger but decided it could benefit them. At least he was talking. She glanced at David, and he gave a slight nod to show he was recording the conversation on his cell phone. Texas was a one-party consent state, which meant only one individual involved in the conversation had to know it was being recorded. In this case, there were two. Her and David. Brian wasn't required to be informed.

It helped that they were also on the street. Brian had no reasonable expectation of privacy in a public space.

She showed him the ledger. "We know, Brian. Margaret made notes about what was happening at the nursery. She named you specifically."

He stiffened. "What... what are you talking about?"

Gotcha. Noelle kept her tone flat but authoritative. "The fake invoices started after you and Kylie were married. We know you were skimming money from the nursery. Margaret found out. Maybe she confronted you about it—"

"No." The word burst out of him with unexpected force. Then Brian closed his eyes and his shoulders sagged. "Margaret never said a word to me about it." His eyes snapped open and his mouth twisted into a grimace. "I would never have hurt her even if she had."

"Why should we believe you? You were stealing from her."

He licked his lips nervously. "I had a gambling problem for a while. One my wife knows nothing about since I handle our finances. Things got out of hand." He pressed two fingers to the bridge of his nose. "I'm ashamed to admit that, yes, I was stealing from the business to pay off my debts. Another two months and I would've been free and clear."

Brian dropped his hand. "But I never would've hurt Margaret. Not in a million years. If she'd confronted me about the stealing, I would've told her the truth. We didn't always get along, but the one thing we had in common was Kylie. Margaret would've kept my secret to protect her sister from being hurt."

There was a thread of genuineness in his voice. Doubt niggled past Noelle's certainty. From the way David's brow furrowed slightly, he was feeling the same way. Could they be wrong about Brian's involvement?

"Kylie and I told you from the beginning," Brian continued. "Waylon is the only one who had a grudge against Margaret."

"Waylon has an alibi for the time of the murder." David placed his hands on his hips. "He was working at the bar."

Brian snorted. "And you think his employees won't lie for him? What a joke. Waylon is used to wriggling his way out of trouble. He tortured Margaret by constantly accusing her of cheating and financially trying to ruin her. When she left him, he lost it."

Confusion muddled Noelle's thoughts. Was Brian simply trying to throw them off by suggesting Waylon was involved in Margaret's murder? It was possible. Noelle held the other man's gaze. "Kylie said, to her knowledge, Waylon never laid a hand on Margaret."

Brian's lips flattened. "Margaret wouldn't have shared the truth with her baby sister. Like I said, she protected Kylie. But Waylon is no stranger to violence. Just today, he was here, fired up about something. Probably drunk, to boot.

Banging on our front door and demanding to speak to Kylie."

"About what?"

"Don't know. I wasn't here, and she wisely didn't open the door."

"Did Kylie call the police?" David asked.

"No, she called me. By the time I arrived, Waylon was gone. Good thing too, because I wouldn't have hesitated to throw the man off my property."

Noelle didn't like the shift this conversation was taking, but she couldn't ignore Waylon's potential involvement. Had his employees lied about where their boss was on the night of the murder? Maybe.

Then again, bars were busy places. The nursery was only a few miles from the center of town. Waylon could've easily slipped out, killed Margaret, and returned to work without anyone being the wiser. The staff might have genuinely believed he was there, even when he wasn't.

It was a possibility Noelle couldn't ignore. "I'd like to speak to Kylie about what happened this morning."

"She's inside, lying down. The incident with Waylon set off a migraine. She's been under a lot of stress since Margaret died."

"We'll be sensitive, but it's important to get her statement before we talk to Waylon."

Brian hesitated and then nodded. "Wait here. I'll ask her to come out."

He hastened up the driveway and disappeared into the house. Noelle watched him go with a mix of trepidation and confusion. Then she glanced at David. "What do you think?"

He lifted his cowboy hat and scraped a hand through his hair. "I'm not sure what to think. Why would Waylon come after Kylie? It doesn't make sense."

"She's the one who gave his name to the police, accused him of being involved in her sister's death. That's enough to trigger someone like Waylon. His criminal record suggests he uses his fists to solve problems."

David nodded, placing his hat back on his head. "I know. It's one reason I suspected Waylon's involvement in Margaret's murder."

The front door of the Turner house opened and Brian hurried out. His face was drawn with panic. "Kylie isn't anywhere in the house. She's gone."

TWELVE

The next day, exhaustion plagued Noelle as she entered her grandmother's kitchen and made a beeline for the coffee machine resting on the counter. She'd spent most of yesterday afternoon and last night searching for Kylie. To no avail. The woman had vanished.

Or been kidnapped. Her cell phone and purse were still in the house. The back door of the Turners' home led to a small side street running along a drainage creek. Tracking dogs had been brought in, but they lost Kylie's scent near the water as if she'd gotten into a vehicle. Waylon had been pulled into the police station for questioning, but he'd invoked his right to an attorney and they'd been forced to release him.

Noelle poured a cup of coffee. The dark brew worked magic on her sluggish brain. She turned and leaned against the counter. The coffee wasn't the only scent filling the space. Sugar and cinnamon made Noelle's stomach growl. She hadn't eaten since yesterday afternoon. It was after seven in the morning.

Her grandmother ran a rolling pin against some dough. She wore an apron with Mrs. Clause holding a plate of cookies. Her gray hair was perfectly styled and her cheeks were lightly painted with blush.

"What are you making, Granny?" Noelle asked, pushing away from the counter.

Sheila lifted a finger to her lips and then pointed toward the living room. Noelle spotted David sprawled out on the recliner, his cowboy boots still on, hat covering his eyes. The faint sound of his gentle snoring brought a smile to her lips. Someone—probably Sheila—had covered him with a handmade quilt.

"Poor man was up most of the night keeping guard over us since the police were busy searching for Kylie." Sheila dusted flour from her fingers. "He finally fell asleep at daybreak. But only after I assured him I'd wake him immediately if anything concerning happened."

Noelle's heart melted. David proved repeatedly that he was a man of honor who'd protect the innocent.

Sheila came up beside her. "He's a good man."

Noelle glanced down at her grandmother, surprised by the tinge of admonishment in the older woman's tone. "I know."

"Glad to hear you realize it." Sheila returned to the island and sprinkled more flour on the dough before picking up the rolling pin again. Judging from the apples and cinnamon on the counter, she was making an apple pie. "So what do you plan to do about David, dear?"

Shock vibrated through Noelle. "What are you talking about?"

Her grandmother shot her a knowing look. "I'm old, but

I'm not brainless. A blind, deaf bat could tell you and David have feelings for each other. Trouble is, you're stubborn. After this case is over, you'll pack your bags and head back to Memphis, leaving that good man behind."

Noelle's hand tightened on her coffee mug. She wasn't sure there was enough caffeine in the world for this conversation. She was also caught off guard. Her grandmother wasn't one to meddle or butt into Noelle's life.

"I live in Tennessee, Granny. My job is there. David knows that." She narrowed her gaze as she perched on a stool at the island. "You weren't hoping that I would make my stay in town permanent, were you?"

"Actually, I was." Sheila set down the rolling pin with a sigh. She swiped her hands against her apron. "You're not happy in Memphis, Noelle, and haven't been for some time. I'm not one to interfere, but it's breaking my heart to see you so miserable."

A well of emotions rose in Noelle at her grandmother's observation. Tears stung her eyes, and she blinked rapidly to hold them back. How many times had the same thoughts filtered through her own mind?

Too many. Noelle sniffed. "I know something needs to change, but I enjoy working for the FBI. It gives me purpose."

Sheila came around the island and placed a loving hand on Noelle's shoulder. "Do you enjoy working for the FBI? Or is it simply a law enforcement career you want? Because those two aren't the same."

"I don't understand what you're getting at."

Her grandmother sighed. "Your father encouraged you to follow in his footsteps and join the FBI. He was well-meaning, but I'm not sure it's the right career fit for you. Nor is living in the big city." Sheila lowered herself onto the stool next to Noelle. "Your spirit always lit up the moment you arrived in Cutler as a kid. The summers here brought you such happiness. I see that same joy in you now, despite the troubles caused by Margaret's murder."

Her mouth lifted into a small smile. "You're saying I'm a country girl at heart?"

"I am, and there's a way for you to stay here and still work in law enforcement, which is a job you genuinely love."

Understanding dawned. "Join the Cutler Police Department."

Sheila nodded, her white curls bouncing with the movement. "It's worth considering, don't you think?"

Noelle wasn't sure how to feel about the suggestion. A mix of emotions tumbled through her. Fear. Worry. Joy. Leaving the FBI and moving to Cutler would mean changing her whole life. Did she want that? While she wasn't happy with the way things were in Memphis, shifting to a small-town police department might not be the answer either.

Her gaze drifted to David, still sleeping in the recliner. A fresh wave of worries zipped through her mind. Noelle didn't want to change her whole life because of a man. Not even one as deserving as David. She needed to decide for herself what she wanted and then consider how that would affect her relationship with the handsome lawman in the next room.

Noelle shifted her attention back to her grandmother. "I

need to think about it. Pray. I don't want to make any rash decisions."

"That's wise." Sheila patted her shoulder, sympathy and understanding reflected in her expression. "Whatever you decide, dear, I'll always support you. I hope you aren't angry with me for speaking my mind."

"Not at all. You want the best for me. I know that." Noelle hugged her sweet grandmother, inhaling the scents of sugar and home. "Thank you for talking to me." She backed away, her mouth lifting into a smile. "Like you said, I'm prone to stubbornness."

Sheila chuckled. "It's a family trait."

They shared a quiet laugh. Her grandmother handed her a freshly baked scone, and Noelle poured more coffee before slipping into the backyard. The air was frigid but crisp. She zipped up her jacket and sat in a chair on the porch. A set of cardinals danced in the oak tree and a squirrel ran across the grass, a nut in its mouth.

Peaceful. Noelle settled back, letting the stillness of the morning wash over her. It was so different from the hustle and bustle of the city, with honking horns and people yelling. Her grandmother was right. Noelle was a country girl at heart.

But did that mean she should change her career? Her life? It was a lot to consider.

Noelle bowed her head.

Lord, I could use some guidance. Granny is right. I'm not happy in Memphis, but I don't know what to do. Did You lead me here to show me the way?

She continued to speak to God, explaining the conflicting

thoughts in her mind. When Noelle was finished, her spirit felt lighter. She hadn't made a decision, but she'd opened her heart to possibilities and change. It was a step in the right direction.

Noelle's cell phone rang just as she was biting into her scone. She fished the device out of her jacket pocket, where she'd stuck it before coming outside. An unfamiliar number flashed on the screen. Local. She answered it.

"He's going to kill me."

The voice was hushed and whispered, but Noelle instantly recognized it. She shot to her feet. "Kylie, where are you?"

"I can't talk now. Meet me at Campsite 17 in the state park at ten tonight. Don't tell anyone other than David that you're coming. No one else can be trusted."

"Who—"

"It's a matter of life and death, Noelle. Please. Come tonight. I'll tell you everything."

Before Noelle could utter another word, Kylie hung up.

THIRTEEN

David pulled into the parking lot closest to Campsite 17. His muscles were knotted with tension. The night was pitch-black. The moon was hidden behind a wall of clouds as yet another rainstorm rolled through. Drizzle patted the windshield. His vehicle was the only one in the parking lot. He killed the engine. "This feels like a trap."

"I know." Noelle sat in the passenger seat, her curly locks pulled into a low hanging ponytail. "But Kylie sounded desperate. Terrified. I can't in good conscience ignore that."

Of course she couldn't. Neither could David. Which is exactly why they were at the campsite, half an hour before ten, to meet with a woman who was in potential danger.

The real question was: who was Kylie running from?

Her husband? Waylon?

"Aiden has officers keeping watch on Brian and Waylon, right?" Noelle asked, her voice steady and sure. "They can't make a move without us knowing about it."

In theory, that was correct. Officers were watching

Brian's home. Waylon was off tonight and had been spotted going into his apartment above the bar. But the plan wasn't foolproof. Either man could slip out another exit, unseen, just as Kylie had done. David wouldn't take anything for granted.

Not when Noelle's life was on the line.

Her face was shrouded in darkness, but as David's eyes adjusted to the night, her features came into visibility. The slant of her nose, the curve of her cheek. He had the urge to start the car and drive away with her. Noelle was a trained FBI agent, capable of handling herself in dangerous situations, but David wanted to protect her. Always.

They still hadn't talked about their kiss from the other night. What was there to discuss? Noelle had been honest from the beginning. Her life was in Memphis. David's was in Cutler. There was no way to reconcile that.

It was cowardly, perhaps, but he hadn't wanted to face the reality. Not yet. She would be gone from his life in a few days. There was no need to rush the matter. In the meantime... David reached out and took her hand. Noelle's skin was warm and soft, her bones delicate yet strong. So much like the woman herself.

She turned to face him. "Can you lead us in prayer?"

"Absolutely." He paused for a moment, gathering his thoughts. "Lord, we ask that you watch over us. Allow us to be Your servants. Give us the strength to help Kylie and bring Margaret's killer to justice. Amen."

"Amen." Noelle squeezed his hand lightly and then leaned over, brushing her lips across his.

It was a fleeting kiss and featherlight, but David's heart skipped several beats. He wanted to gather her in his arms and hold her. Kiss her until they were both breathless and lost in each other. But now wasn't the time. Not with a potential killer tracking their moves and a scared woman waiting in the campsite.

Instead, he squeezed her hand back before reluctantly releasing her. Then he removed his weapon from its holster and checked the clip one last time. Fully loaded. His backup weapons—a knife and a smaller handgun—were strapped to his ankles. Measure after measure. Necessary ones since they didn't know what they were walking into.

Was Kylie involved in her sister's murder? Working with her husband or someone else? It was a possibility. David snapped the magazine back into his Glock and holstered it before turning to Noelle. "Ready?"

She nodded, reaching for the door handle. "Let's do this."

The night air was biting as David exited the SUV. He zipped up his coat, his gaze sweeping the immediate area. This campsite was off the beaten path and therefore more suitable for experienced outdoorsmen. The parking lot abutted a worn and narrow path through the woods. A handmade wooden sign directed visitors with an arrow to a cabin buried in the trees.

Unease settled in the space between David's shoulder blades as he stepped onto the path. Branches reached for his clothes and face like claws. Somewhere overhead, an owl hooted. He kept his hand on his weapon inside its holster, ready to draw at a moment's notice. Noelle followed behind. Their footsteps were muffled by the thick layer of leaves coating the ground. Raindrops bounced off the tree branches, the cold water dampening his face and coat.

Something scurried in the bushes. David's heart leapt into his throat, and he froze. A dark shape the size of a rabbit or a raccoon raced across the path before disappearing into the trees.

David breathed out. The condensed air hung in front of his face for a moment before evaporating. He willed his heart to slow down and focused on the sounds of the surrounding forest. If someone was out there, he couldn't hear them moving. Yet something made the hair on the back of his neck stand on end. Nothing about this felt right.

"Stay close," he whispered to Noelle. "The cabin is just ahead."

She planted a hand on his back in response. Together, in tune, they continued forward. The trees parted, revealing a rustic cabin. No lights were on inside. Not even from the glow of a candle or flashlight. It looked deserted.

Was Kylie inside hiding? Or had she lured them here for a nefarious purpose?

David stilled. It was quiet. He circled the building with Noelle, keeping inside the shelter of the trees. There was only one way in and out of the cabin. Through the front door. He leaned close to Noelle's ear and whispered, "Cover me. I'm going to see if Kylie is inside."

She nodded, unholstering her weapon and holding it with ease. Her expression was fierce. Powerful. David trusted Noelle fully to watch his back. It was her duty, yes, but there was more to it than that. Their connection was a partnership in every sense of the word.

They protected each other. Supported each other.

Loved one another.

The thought jolted David. Love? Was he falling in love with Noelle?

The questions tumbled through his mind, a distraction he couldn't afford at the moment. He needed to focus. David breathed in and then out, letting his muscles relax as he tuned his senses to their surroundings one last time.

Silence.

He pulled his own weapon and stepped into the small clearing. In three strides, David was at the cabin's front door. He listened for a moment before stealing a peek inside the window. It was dark inside. Rain dripped down the collar of his jacket, dampening his shirt collar. Thunder rumbled like a warning in the distance.

He glanced over his shoulder, but Noelle wasn't visible in the trees. He felt her presence, though, and knew she was watching him and the surrounding woods. David grasped the door handle. The metal was frigid against his palm. A prayer on his lips, he twisted the knob.

The hinges creaked as the door opened. David peeked around the jamb, but the cabin inside was pitch-black. Lumps that resembled furniture were barely discernible. He shoved the door open wider with his foot and entered the structure, gun leading the way. "Kylie? Are you here? It's David Carpenter."

No response. Dread gripped him as he moved farther inside. Shapes formed as his eyes adjusted to the darkness. The cabin was one room. A couch and coffee table in front of an unlit fireplace. Bunk beds. A tiny kitchen. He lowered his weapon.

The interior of the cabin was warm, and David crossed the room. He held out a hand toward the hearth. Heat radiated from the logs, which had recently been doused. Someone had been here within the last half hour or so.

He rose. His hiking boot kicked something on the floor, sending it skittering along the cement. It smacked into an object hidden in a nook near the bunk beds. It glowed an eerie red.

What on earth? David peered at the shapeless mass, but couldn't pinpoint what he was looking at. He drew closer and bent down, his fingers brushing against cloth. A blanket? He lifted it, revealing the object underneath.

His breath stalled. A bomb. Simple. Like the kind someone could learn to make on the internet.

It had a timer. Ticking down.

20 seconds.

David shot to his feet and bolted across the room. His heart thundered in his ears. The world narrowed to the doorway of the cabin. His escape route. But exiting the structure likely wouldn't be enough. The explosion from the bomb would send shrapnel and remnants of the rustic cabin far and wide.

Noelle.

He had to warn her. David added more fuel to his legs and burst from the cabin. Noelle was a dark shape in the cleaning. He sucked in a deep breath and shouted, "Bomb!"

She froze for half a moment before turning toward the forest and running. He caught up with her at the tree line. A wave of white heat shoved him with the same effectiveness as a set of invisible hands. David's arms shot out, wrapping Noelle in his embrace as they tumbled to the earth. Something hard hit the back of his head.

Everything went black.

FOURTEEN

Noelle lay stunned on the ground for three heartbeats as her lungs tried to remember to work. Ash and wood pieces fell around her. The cabin was a ball of flames. It took far too long to realize that the reason she couldn't draw breath was because David's heavy form was crushing her. He lay motionless. His arms cradled her protectively but were limp.

Her heart skittered. "David?"

He didn't move. She wriggled in an attempt to dislodge him. Something warm and wet coated her neck. Noelle's fingers touched the liquid, and in the light of the flames, she made out the color.

Blood.

Not hers. His.

"David!" Panic she couldn't control or reason with infused her voice.

He groaned. Short-term relief gave way to new worry. He was injured. How badly? Noelle shoved, and he rolled off her onto the soggy ground. The rain was picking up speed, tapping her insistently. She ignored the damp cold. With shaking fingers, Noelle explored David's face, neck, and head, tripping over a cut buried in his thick hair. It was large and already swelling.

David tried to shake off her ministrations and sat up. "Are you hurt?"

"No." Noelle did a quick assessment of her own limbs. Everything worked, although her body would be sore for days after colliding with the ground. "You've got a goose egg on the back of your head. Probably a concussion to go with it."

He glowered at the now-destroyed cabin. "Kylie set us up."

"It looks like it." She reached for her phone and dialed Aiden's number, requesting backup. The police chief promised officers were en route along with an ambulance. Noelle hung up. "Help is on the way."

She lifted her jacket and tore a piece of fabric from her undershirt. Blood was running from David's wound, coating the collar of his jacket. She needed to slow it down. Noelle pressed the cloth to the wound. Head injuries were dangerous. They could be deadly.

Fear, unlike any she'd ever known, coursed through her veins. If David hadn't made it out of the cabin... she would've lost him. It was a terrifying prospect, and it brought Noelle's life—her wants and desires—into startling clarity.

A woman's scream echoed through the night. It was pure terror.

Then it abruptly cut off.

Noelle's breath hitched. Her gaze met David's, the same

question running through her mind reflected in his eyes. She glanced at the burning cabin, rising to her feet. "Was that Kylie?"

David braced himself against a tree and also stood. "Maybe." His brow creased. "Someone was in the cabin until a little while ago. The logs in the fireplace were still warm. The killer may have beaten us to her."

Worry for the other woman gripped Noelle. There wasn't a moment to waste. "Stay here. I'm going to find her."

"Not a chance." David grabbed her arm with surprising strength. "We'll go together."

She hesitated and then nodded. David was hurt but on his feet. Nothing would dissuade him from coming with her, and there wasn't time to argue. She prayed his head wound was minor.

Noelle adjusted the hold on her weapon and motioned for David to follow her. Together, they entered the path leading to the creek. Noelle's breath came in bursts as she ran. Roots threatened to trip her. Lightning bolted across the sky and the rain increased. Her hair became plastered to her head. Water dripped into her eyes, blurring her already poor visibility.

Behind her, David barked out orders to someone on the phone. Backup. But would anyone get there in time? Likely not. Noelle mentally berated herself for listening to Kylie in the first place about having other police officers involved. It'd been a mistake not to bring backup to the campsite, but Kylie had been so scared… so certain that involving anyone else would put her life at risk. Cutler was a small town. Gossip ran quick. Perhaps Kylie was afraid of this exact scenario. Her location discovered by the killer.

A break in the trees appeared. Noelle slowed down but kept moving. All at once, she was deposited on the bank of a creek. The nearby water bubbled and gurgled. A man's voice drifted downstream. Lightning blazed the sky, illuminating the bridge several yards away. Noelle gasped.

Larry Paulson held Kylie at gunpoint.

A hand grabbed Noelle, tugging her behind the shelter of a tree. David. His breathing was ragged, his features tight with pain. He gritted his teeth. "Stay down. He doesn't know we're alive, and we need to use that to our advantage."

David was right. She peeked around the tree bark. Larry had Kylie against the railing of the bridge. Why hadn't he shot her? Noelle couldn't come up with a reasonable explanation, but Larry was smart enough to have a plan.

Noelle took aim but had no shot. "There's no way to take him out from here. I have to get closer."

"There's another bridge downstream, about a quarter of a mile away. I'll cross and double back. We can block him in."

Another wave of worry gripped her. Noelle snagged the fabric of David's sleeve before he could take off. "You're injured. I'll go."

"You won't be able to find the bridge. It's hidden and not well used. I know these woods like the back of my hand."

David reached up and touched her cheek. His fingers were ice cold. Lightning brightened the sky once more, revealing the stark amount of blood coating his jacket. He was hurt worse than he let on.

"We're made for this, Noelle." His lips curled up in the briefest smile. "Let's catch this killer and go home."

With those parting words, David disappeared into the woods, taking her heart with him.

Noelle sent up a prayer for his safety before setting her gaze back on the bridge, and the couple engaged in some kind of argument. The park had placed safety lights on the bridge, providing illumination that served as a warning or guidance to hikers traversing in the dark.

Kylie was in the center of the bridge. She clung to the railing. Terror was etched across her features, and something dangled from her wrists. Rope? It appeared ragged and torn, as if she'd sawed the binds free.

Larry stood just past her, closer to the north side of the woods, holding a gun. His face was mottled with rage as he stalked closer to Kylie. "No one is coming to save you. Didn't you see the cabin blow up?"

Noelle crept closer, using the darkness and shadows to hide her approach. She raised her gun and took aim again, but frustratingly, the angle was all wrong. She couldn't hit Larry without risking Kylie.

"Please." Tears streaked down Kylie's face. "I called Noelle and arranged the meeting. You promised to spare my life if I did what you said."

That explained some things. Larry had kidnapped Kylie and used her to draw Noelle and David to the park. He'd intended to kill all of them with the bomb, but Kylie escaped.

Kylie edged toward Noelle's side of the bridge. "Please, Larry. We're childhood friends. You promised to spare my life if I did as you said."

"I lied." His voice was deadly flat, despite the deep hatred creasing his features. His dark hair clung to his head and his glasses were gone. "You stole from me. You and Margaret. Did you really think I was going to let you get away with it?"

The loan. Larry had given Margaret and Kylie money to keep their business afloat, and then he'd discovered that someone was embezzling when he reviewed the financial documents. He'd confronted Margaret about it. She hadn't known what he was talking about.

Because she was innocent. And so was Kylie.

Larry lifted his gun, intending to shoot. Noelle's gaze arced to the woods behind him, but there was no sign of David. Had he collapsed while running to the other bridge? Or was he still on the way? She had no way of knowing.

She was also out of time.

Noelle burst free of the tree line. "Police! Larry, put your weapon down."

In a flash, he grabbed Kylie and held his gun to her head. Larry's face twisted into a sneer. "You're supposed to be dead."

"I'm not that easy to kill." She kept her weapon pointed at the criminal. "Put the gun down and let Kylie go. We can all walk out of this alive."

Kylie was wide-eyed with terror. Tears streaked her face and her teeth chattered violently. Larry had an arm wrapped around her waist, holding her tight against him. The barrel of his weapon was pressed against Kylie's temple. He took a step away from Noelle. "I'm not going to jail."

"That's something we can discuss once you let Kylie go and put the gun down."

He took another step toward the woods on the opposite side of the bridge, dragging Kylie with him. "She stole from me!"

"No, she didn't." Noelle kept her tone steady and nonconfrontational.

In the shadows, a form appeared.

David.

Noelle's relief at the sight of him was short-lived. He was creeping up behind Larry, but one false move and the criminal would shoot Kylie. Noelle had to keep Larry's focus on her. "Brian was the one embezzling money from the nursery. He's been doing it for years. Neither Kylie nor Margaret had any idea."

Larry's eyes widened. "You're lying."

Noelle kept moving closer. "No, I'm not. Brian admitted it to us. We have his confession recorded." Her boots slid against the wood of the bridge. A few more inches and she could grab Kylie. "Brian had a gambling problem for many years. He hid it from everyone and was creating fake invoices to steal money from the nursery to pay back his debts."

David was closing in too. Noelle avoided looking at him in case she accidentally alerted Larry to his presence. Instead, she kept her entire focus on the criminal in front of her. "Now's the opportunity to do the right thing, Larry. Kylie was telling you the truth when she denied any involvement in the embezzlement. Let her go."

He wavered. Tears shimmered in his eyes.

Noelle held his gaze. "Let your childhood friend go."

Larry began lowering the weapon from Kylie's temple when David's boot scraped against the wood plank of the bridge. Noelle snagged Kylie's wrist and pulled the woman toward her as Larry spun.

David tackled him. The two men fell to the ground in a tangle of limbs.

A gunshot erupted.

FIFTEEN

Three days later

"Larry Paulson will go to prison for a very long time." Aiden slapped a file folder on his desk. The leather chair creaked as he settled his form into it. Sunshine streamed in through the window behind him. Main Street was bustling, residents doing their last-minute shopping. It was Christmas Eve. "Once I presented all the evidence we'd gathered against him, Larry confessed to Margaret's murder and the attacks on Noelle."

David's spine relaxed. The stitches in his head ached, but nothing could steal away his relief at knowing Larry wouldn't see the outside of a prison cell again. He glanced at Noelle, seated in the other visitor's chair. Curly strands framed her beautiful face and the smile on her lips. Aiden's news erased the last of the worry lines from her forehead.

She caught his gaze and reached out to take his hand. David interlaced their fingers, ignoring the faint arching of his boss's eyebrows. "Did Larry explain what happened on the night he killed Margaret?"

"Yes. He hid his vehicle on the farm road because he wasn't sure if Kylie and Brian were working and didn't want them to know he was meeting Margaret. He threatened to go to the police about the embezzlement. During the conversation, Larry grew angry. He took the scissors from the front desk. Then he followed Margaret into the rear of the store and killed her."

Regret punched David's heart. "Margaret called me because of the embezzlement?"

"Probably. She must've suspected Larry intended to go to the police and wanted to figure out how much trouble Brian would be in."

"What about Kylie and Brian?" Noelle asked. "What happens to them?"

"We've cleared them both of Margaret's murder. Brian confessed to stealing from the nursery, but as owner, Kylie would have to press charges in order for him to be prosecuted for the embezzlement. She won't do that." Aiden folded his hands. "As for luring you two out to the campsite, Kylie had been kidnapped and terrorized by Larry. She was desperate to save her own life."

"Of course she was." Noelle's tone held no condemnation. "She's apologized several times. Not that it was necessary. Larry is the one to blame for everything that happened. I'm just grateful no one else got hurt."

So was David. Those last moments on the bridge, before Larry was in custody, were harrowing. The killer's gun went off while David was wrestling for control of the weapon, but fortunately, the shot went wide. No one was injured.

"What about Waylon?" David asked. "Why did he show up at Kylie's house, yelling and screaming?"

"He was drunk and angry about something regarding the funeral." Aiden scratched his chin. "In his own twisted way, I think Waylon loved Margaret. He was devastated by her death but hid it well. I've convinced him to see a counselor. I think it'll help."

They reviewed a bit more about the case and Aiden had them sign some final reports. Then he extended his hand toward Noelle. "It's been a pleasure working with you. If you're ever in need of a job, our door is always open."

She smiled. "Thank you, Chief. I'll keep that in mind."

David shook his boss's hand as well, and Aiden patted him on the back. "Job well done. Now don't come back into the station until after the New Year. Doctor's orders."

His mouth quirked. "I wouldn't have come today, but you called me in."

Aiden laughed. "Smart aleck. Get out of my office."

"Give my love to Holly."

"Will do."

David followed Noelle through the bull pen and out into the crisp air. She wrapped a scarf around her neck. This one was a faded pink that accented the color in her cheeks and the natural shade of her kissable lips. He tucked his hands in the pockets of his jacket to keep from reaching for her. "You leave town the day after Christmas, huh?"

"I'm supposed to." She jutted her chin toward the coffee shop nearby. "Mind joining me for a caffeine fix?"

"Sure." He offered Noelle his arm, and she tucked her

hand into the crook of his elbow. They strolled down Main Street. Several residents called out hello. The Christmas tree in the square was lit up. A beacon of holiday cheer. Joy tangled with sadness in David's chest. This moment with Noelle was bittersweet. A glimpse of what life could be like for them, but it wasn't fair to ask her to stay in Cutler. She had a career and a life in Memphis.

He was resolved to let her go with grace. Her happiness was all he wanted.

The coffee shop was packed. Noelle snagged a table in the rear while David got their drinks. He sat in the chair next to her, back to the wall. This area of the shop was behind a set of winding stairs. It shielded them from the hustle of the front counter. Holiday music played softly over the speakers.

Noelle accepted her coffee with a smile. "Thanks." She shifted in her seat and glanced around the shop before her gaze settled on him. "There's something I wanted to talk to you about."

"Okay." Nerves jittered in his stomach.

"I've been doing a lot of thinking lately. About me. About my job." She fiddled with the plastic top on her coffee. "About us."

Of its own accord, his hand came to rest on her forearm. "Noelle... you don't have to say anything. It's okay. You've been honest from the beginning that your future is in Tennessee and with the FBI." David drew in a steadying breath. "I care about you. Deeply. I think... well, I'm falling in love with you all over again. Trouble is, I can't leave Cutler. My family is here. My life is here. I love this town and the residents in it. The big city isn't for me. Which is why I completely understand your need to return to Memphis. That's where your life is. I would never ask you to give it up."

Tears filmed her beautiful eyes. "Granny was right. You are a good man, David."

He couldn't resist bopping her nose lightly with his finger. "You discussed me with your grandmother?"

She laughed lightly, which was the reaction David hoped for. "Actually, Granny lectured me, if I'm being honest. But the words were something I needed to hear."

"I don't understand."

She turned toward him and took a deep breath. "I'm not happy in Memphis and haven't been for some time. Law enforcement is my calling, but my job with the FBI requires so much of my time and energy. I'm drained. Part of the reason for my trip to Cutler was to figure out what changes needed to happen in my life." She met his gaze. "Granny was the one who pointed out that I'm a country girl at heart. And she's right. Some of my best childhood memories were made in this town. And with you."

David's breath stalled in his chest. He froze, afraid to move and break the moment.

Noelle's gaze was warm. "I'm going back to Memphis after Christmas and quitting my job. I'm moving to Cutler." Her lips lifted in a smile. "I want to build a life here and I was really hoping you'd like to be a part of it."

He almost couldn't believe his ears. David leaned forward and kissed her, pouring all of his emotions into it while still mindful that they were in a public place. Then he rested his forehead against hers.

"Are you sure, Noelle? Margaret's murder case was

unusual for this town." His chest tightened, the accusation from his ex ringing in his ears. Dependable David. "You might get bored. Of here. And of me."

Her fingertips traced his jaw. "I've never been more sure of anything. Cutler is home. It's a place where I can build friendships and community. Get married. Have a family. I want excitement, but not the kind we've had for the last few days. I want stable, dependable tranquility."

Noelle touched his bottom lip, her gaze lifting to meet his. "I'm falling in love with you too, David. You were my best friend as a kid. Now you're the man I can count on. The one who supports me but also makes my heart race with a single touch. There's nothing more precious than that."

Her words were like a balm to his worries. David captured her hand in his and placed a kiss on the inside of her palm. "Do you think tonight is too soon for our first date?"

She leaned back, mischief lighting her eyes. "I hope not. Now hurry and finish your coffee. All this murder and mayhem means I haven't done a lick of Christmas shopping." She wriggled her eyebrows. "Anything in particular on your list?"

He grinned, his heart light and happy, and brushed a kiss against her mouth once more. "I've already got everything I could've asked for."

ALSO BY LYNN SHANNON

Texas Ranger Heroes Series

Ranger Protection

Ranger Redemption

Ranger Courage

Ranger Faith

Ranger Honor

Triumph Over Adversity Series

Calculated Risk

Critical Error

Necessary Peril

Would you like to know when my next book is released? Or when my novels go on sale? It's easy. Subscribe to my newsletter at www.lynnshannon.com and all of the info will come straight to your inbox!

Reviews help readers find books. Please consider leaving a review at your favorite place of purchase or anywhere you discover new books. Thank you.

Manufactured by Amazon.ca
Bolton, ON

41336944R00065